Heapatrouble

Novels by D.D. Cross

A Den of Brigands

Field of Corns

Back to Hades: Eustice Seeney Returns to Hell

Go to Hell! (I DID) Interview with Eustice Seeney

Heapatrouble

Heapatrouble

D.D. Cross

MMA

Publishing

D.D. CROSS

All rights reserved under International and Pan-American Copyright Conventions. Published by the MMA Publishing Group International.

ISBN-13: 978-0615748313
ISBN-10: 0615748317

Cover Art by Yuri Nasso

Printed in the United States of America

10 9 8 7 6 5 4 3 2 1

HEAPATROUBLE

A Handbook of Curious Imaginations, Uncomfortable Observations, and Bizarre and Grotesque Mischief

Doctor Wiley's Disclaimer

My name is Trip Wiley. I'm a fallen medical doctor, somewhat mad, often disoreiented, (we'll get back to that) and every bit a true scientist in the empirical manner. I have had the acquaintance of Eustice Seeney for over two decades, and can attest to his afterlife experience. Seeney was declared clinically dead, kept on life support for organ harvest, and spontaneously recovered. I was his attending physician when the cocksucker died again. You see, after his first death and resurrection I wrote a series of articles, which were published in scientific literature. Unfortunately they brought disdain and accusations, ultimately resulting in me just saying fuck it all, and I did. The second dying of Seeney brought even more headaches, and I figured there wasn't much to lose so I went along with his crypitc will. I actually came face to face with Mr. Mephistopheles himself hence; the regimen of altered states, primarily to numb my mind from the hideous nature of my experiences. Disorientation didn't remain a viable alternative to reality, as described in an entire treatise, created by a very clever author who invented Eustice and me too. But that's irrelevant in light of the following events. Just to be clear let me state the following for the record:

Eustice Seeney died, went to hell, managed to escape, and in return he swore to make ammeds. To who, what, or why? Well Eustice will tell you that. These are some of Eustice's adventures on earth. The stories you're about to read are of the lives he invented, and may give you a new way of looking at the ordinary, banal, and of course the truly hideous and groesque. I just tried to keep Eustice from a premature demise, and remain,

Sincerely Yours,

Trip Wiley, M.D.

So much for that, right?

EUSTICE SEENEY

Howdy Doody folks. Heaven and hell. Yep there's a whole lot of stuff these days about the two. Mostly folks take to jibber jabberin' about the former rather than the latter. Satan's special social club, H E double hockey sticks, HELL!

I reckon you sell more books talkin' about all the nicey nice things that happen to you if you up and die, instead of what really does happen to some of us. That bugs me like a collsarn earworm from a bad jingle about some car insurance company, or cheeseburger shop. I get to lookin' at the internet and it seems like every month or so some whizz bang expert got some story about the bright white lights, and all the la ti da'ness that comes along with bein' dead. Listen up: dead's dead. There's always some strings attached, and the expert usually ends up makin' some pert near fine bank from their tellin'. And it's always like I said: about goin' to Heaven.

Bleah. I tell you bleah to the Nth degree. Readin' about all this preachy stuff makes every cell in my body up and vomit till they're all shrivelled up into dried molecular apricots.

A spell back I died on the operatin' table, went to hell, and managed to survive. I got to tell my story to a smart compassionate doc, who got hisself in some real trouble, on account he'd said stuff that'd make a virgin's hymen grow back. We only got a brief spot on the Leno show, and if you don't get the words out now there ain't no later. I ain't never heard of no dead folks talkin', and if I did it'd give me the hibbidy jibbidies so bad I'd end up in a looney bin. Of course there's that fella on the cross. But that's a whole different story.

From Vegas Without Much Love
Trip Wiley's Backstory

I'd pretty much blown whatever chances I had of my life returning to normalcy after I broke Eustice out of the hospital, stole an ambulance, and ran off to Las Vegas with one of the nurses, but that's what I did.

I left Eustice and headed to sin city in the corporeal world. I actually came face to face with the most sinister source of evil on earth. I remain convinced that it was Satan because Eustice Seeney did die, and all accounts of his experience were documented. The fact's are indisputible. I stand by the position that the Satan I crossed paths with was indeed a force unlike any other. There is no human being that could have access to so much instantaneous information, the power to bring about meteorological events, and profound changes to the world. Certainly it could be disputed, that my experience was under duress and influenced by other vectors. But I witnessed a human being move the planet. Even if I sound as crazy as any other whack job that claims to see little green men, so be it. I'd had it with the paranormal. After springing Eustice, dueling the Devil, and all the craziness that came along with it, I had to split. I was in no position to cope with the earthly forces of law enforcemnt. Hell, I'd be sent off to some pscych ward, and held until trial for the wake of destruction.

Eustice's emergence from his second coma, the maniacal chase by this Satanic figure, and the nurse he kidnapped, was far too much to explain to some bumpkin law enforcment agents. The nurse, she had enough abuse at the hands of this monster. He delved into every aspect of her life like some super powered Facebook. The ability to tamper wtih her unborn children not only frazzled her, but hammered in the fact that the man I encountered, and Eustice escaped from, was Satan himself.

So we, Nurse Martinez and I, headed out for Vegas to drown our cosmic debris: the remains of Satan in some very human, very silly, human debauchery. And the best place to do it was "Sin City" itself.

Eustice could and probably will tell you all about the constructs of hell. How it's not just a geographical location, but some interdimensional locale populated by souls, who for one reason or another found themselves damned. I don't want to get into some metaphysical mumbo jumbo, but I learned that there is a tremendous force that's governed by an inside-out set of rules. It is controlled by a creature, who watches each and every keystroke of the computer, every web site you visit, and has eyes through every lense. Keeping tabs in some grand galactic machination more intricate and diverse than my conceptual ceiling can grasp. We'll get back to some of that later.

So there I was in Las Vegas. Nurse Martinez lasted a few weeks with all the ruckus before deciding to return to Miami and her husband. Yeah, he'd been cuckholded, but Ronda Martinez RN was confident he'd take her back. Our "fling" was more a decompression from a profound blast of surreal, monstrous madness, and she grew tired of round-the-clock boozing, crap tables, and Elvis impersonators. The relationship wasn't going anywhere, and me? Hell. I didn't know that Eustice had made things right for me. He had plenty of money left from his last lawsuit, and lawyers on retainer. So my name was somewhat cleared. There was some probationary status, but nothing so severe that leaving Las Vegas would be something to shed a tear over.

I called Eustice, and he pleaded with me to come join him at his new facility saving souls. He said he'd gotten it all squared away as a legitimate agency, and had an office. I had nothing except an old car, mutton chop side burns, and a wardrobe out of a bad movie. I'd been working as an Elvis impersonator to keep a roof over my head, and the motel was already asking for rent, which I had already fallen into arears.

So there it is. My trip back to Florida and working at the Center Eustice had going.

Eustice Seeney's office was on the second floor of what might have been considered a modern medical building thirty years ago. The neighborhood, with its labyrinths of interconnecting suites may once have been home to some of the finest experts and professionals, but they were long gone. In its place were mail order naturopaths, chiropractors, massage therapists (of the happy ending sort), and a host of off kilter types. Many whom, likely had regular appointments with their probation officers.

Seeney's Soul Salvation Center had a huge glass door with the initials SSC, and the phrase: Hell Can Wait!

I thought the exclamation point a bit much, but hey. It's not every day a guy who's kicked twice, finagled his way out of his own heck, offers to jump start your battery. As for me, I wasn't just in need of a jump, I needed a Die Hard. The fact that Seeney sent a classic nineteen 'fifty-nine' Cadillac convertible, a duplicate of the one I'd wrecked, and had it waiting for me at Fort Lauderdale airport bode good things could very well be on the horizon. What the hey?

I took a seat across from him, looked at the man and said: "It took some time to get here. I guess I'm ready to go to work."

I was curious as to why he chose this particular part of the world to set up shop, and this is what I discovered:

Eustice wandered the country for forty days and forty nights, or so he said. Upon his arrival at the mythical city of Golden Springs, a town, which had once been part of the American Dream, he awoke to a nightmare of a nice little town gone bad.

Because Eustice suffered significant harm from a series of medical errors occurring at Thompson Memorial Hospital in Miami, Florida, there was no shortage of attorneys. It took little time to settle his list of claims out of court. Eustice, grateful to have survived a laundry list of miscalculations, medical negligence, and a host of highly suspicious criminal acts, did not want to have his day in court. However, the lawyer he chose, one very slick, crafty, and most eloquent barrister, maneuvered a hefty settlement. The series of events that left Seeney in a coma, declared dead, and kept warm for organ harvesting, was his second experience as such at the same hospital in so many years. They could not afford another onslaught of litigation. Too many staffers were involved, and the term "policy limits payout" would bankrupt the hospital.

His coffers were brimming, and as a tax exempt charity, ordained minister, and someone intent on making wrong right, Eustice was good to go. I hoped that this would be a less than strenuous venture, and I could find plenty of time to catch up on my daytime TV, exercise, and maybe meet a nice girl. The divorce set me back quite a bit, and I wouldn't mind making a few scoots either. So here I am, watching television, waiting for the next commercial, and wondering if things will work out.

Hang on. I hear someone calling....It's Eustice. I think he has something, make that everything, to have an opinion on.

DUMBNESSTUDE
STUPID is contagious and is spread by the TV (Eustice)

Doc Wiley got the TV on so loud I can nary hear my thinker brain's thoughts. Hang on: "Turn that collsarn thing down Doc!"

That's better, thanks. Hey folks I got me to thinkin' about how loud the commercials are on TV. F'rinstance you can be watchin' a show, and all of a sudden...the decibels go on up so loud your collsarn ear drums start achin'. I know everyone's got somethin' to sell, and they, the sellin' people got to figurin' the best way to do it is by annoying you. That there is wrong. Wrong, wrong, wrong. My solution's simple I take a cord to a TV set, at every home I visit and cut it. This is called "cord cuttin'" and what it does is prevent Satan's message from gettin' into your home.

Satan's Message?

That's the sort of question I get a lot. Folks look at me like I'm some sort a crazy fella, but I know the evil that comes between you enjoying the aesthetical aspects of a fine TV show or movie is spoiled by an intervening commercial. All the folks who've died and gone to hell know that TV commercials were the invention of Ole Mister Mephistopheles himself.

You see back in the twentieth century when television was just getting invented folks, who had things to sell spend their load of capital on ways to advertise more effectively than billboards. Don't nobody remember them billboards? How `bout barns that had Red Man Chewin' Terbacky on `em? Yep there was plenty of visual ads back then, and then came radio. Hoowee they used to have a heckuva lot of folks listenin' to music. Nowadays there's more commercials on radio than there is on TV.

Just to put things in context: Radio? That there was Satan's first subliminal message transmitter. Ole Satan would sneak in secret phrases to make people think bad thoughts. Sin signals whilst they was drivin' and layin' in bed with the radio on. Old Elvis be having a song sung, next thing there'd be some sody pop commercial interlaced with secret messages that'd drive people to foul deeds. Back in the hippy days they'd play these long songs, and then there'd be a commercial that sounded real smooth that was really some demonic message. Look at all those youngens that took to the drugs, and the communisms, Hellsfire. There was all that free love goin' on, and that was on account there was secret messages tellin' gals to toss their undies in the trash and get it on with strangers. Yep. I remember them days, on account I still had to pay for MY painted ladies. Then came the days of the disco. I can't even get into how many secretic messages Satan tied in there. I reckon there'd been so much qualudin' and cocainin' that people got to doin' so much stuff they all landed right slam dunk in Hades. Hellsfire. You ain't got to look much farther than the famous athletes, who took to the drugs back then and ended up damned.

So gettin' back to commercials on TV, today, most folks have gotten smart and switched to cable, or even that cable radio too.

My job's been to turn down the volume of the world. Startin with the radios and TV, right on down to a bare whisper so you don't get them secret demonic messages in your ear. You sure's don't wanta catch none of Satan's brainworms them is killers. They lay eggs that hatch, and next thing you know you're whole thinker brain's crawlin' with dopey ass ideas, thoughts, and ruminations. I been pert well successful without even tryin' too much. I think commercials do a lot onto themselves on account, they just tick people off and the channel gets changed. Ain't nobody likes havin' someone tellin' them what to do. Hell no.

That there's just a sample of how Satan sneaks into everyday life, tweaks this or that, and next thing you know, you're damned for eternity.

I think they was tryin' to ban loud commercials from them cookin' channels a spell back, on account foul messages tend to make folks throw up too much. Ain't nobody likes seein' somebody do the rainbow yawn. Hell no!

So be careful what you listen to because without a filter you might just get the wrong message. I recommend earmuffs year round. And we just so happen to have them for sale at the Eustice Seeney Soul Salvation Center. I'd say to get `em on online, but the problem is that we can't figure out how to cut out the middle guys, I think they's Satanic. You know that duo the Italian and Hebrew guys? Old Mr. Shipiro and Handelini. We're workin' on it.

SHIPPIN' and HANDLIN'
Mission #238SH

I knew these folk was sinners. Didn't know where they was, so when I got over to the Soul Salvation Center had a good idea what my next chore was, and that my dear heathenistical friends was to find out who them people was, and bring `em to the light.

Ole Doc Wiley was sittin' around the office, and I gotta tell you he's one durn lazy sumbitch. He had my Early Times bottle out and a glass in his hand. There he was sippin' away the day, startin' bright and early at 9 a.m.

"Collsarn it doc, what in tarnation are you doin'?" I said. Had my fists all clenched up, ready on account I gotta show some muscle. I am in need of a few weeks at the gym, make that months. Anyway, he takes a gulp, looks up from the glass and says:

"Eustice, how's it going man?"

"Wiley, we got us some work to do now. Git yourself movin' over to the phone book."

We used phone books not computers here at the SSC. You know why? OLE Satan's watchin' every keystroke, every website, and we ain't lettin' that Devil in on what we're up to. No siree. We don't even use them cell phones, but for nothin' that can be tracked, traced, or trailed. Uhn uh.

I get to figgerin' the guys Shippin' and Handlin' got to run the world. They're on everything, everywhere, and they make lots and lots of money.

I figure one's an Italian fella, and the other's a Hebrew. I don't reckon it'd be too difficult to track `em down, and figure I'd pop in on some kin.

I started with all the Ship families. I figure Shipolito, Shiponi, maybe Shipiro, or something like that. I get Doc Wiley to check out the Handlings: Handlino, Handlingberg, Handel, Handini, and on and on. Lot's of folks to check out. We got our work cut out.

I'll get back at you when we narrow it down.

Oh yeah, what are we supposed to do when we find `em? Well, I reckon set up a foundation sort of thing to get some folks out of Hades. What do you think? I'm up for suggestions cause I ain't so sure yet myself. I'll get back at ya.

Trip Wiley's Position
...You gotta be kidding-

I wasn't particularly keen on investigating an obviously idiotic notion. No, not one bit. In fact working for Eustice is torture. If I just playing along I can get paid for doing nothing, drink if I like, get high, and maybe check out the women. That does read rather sadly as a testament. I do come off as a cad of sorts, but what can I say? I left Vegas at the lowest point in my life: broke, beaten, soon-to-be divorced. Yes, I had a wife in Australia, who had been less than thrilled with my going back to America, but I did. I cheated on her, and stayed long enough to help Eustice when he was in the hospital. Above all, losing my medical license again, being fined, and ultimately banished from medical practice. You see, Eustice, is my uncle by marriage, and in some twisted way I felt compelled to join him on whatever endeavor he set out on.

How in the world am I supposed to look into a concept? Shipping and handling...Jeez, the things I do for Seeney. I guess the best way to go about this is to simply lie.

Mission Ridiculous
Or: Light the flatulence.and kick the tires...

I don't particularly care for talkin' 'bout folks who are near that long snaky tunnel leadin' right on down to hell, unless I could help 'em. But there's one case I had to turn down. Some folks just ain't got no redeemin' qualities at all. Nope. None whatsoever.

There's this old gal, who'd been married to a fella for some sixty years or so. Old folks on their way on out. I'd have to reckon they lived a decent enough life, that they got themselves all nice and settled, and had things-as far as the corporeal world goes, set just fine.

But that tweren't the case. This is what happened: One day the old man was sittin', watchin' the TV, and there's a knock on the door. It's John Q Law, a lawyer, and some men in white suits. They set out to puttin' the old fella in a looney bin. Hoowee, that was one hornswaggle. The old gal got this fella locked up and out of the way, so she could go about her life just as she saw fit.

Now the children they had was all growed. One lived east, another west, and some in parts unknown. From what I gathered there weren't too much fuzzy family business. Your typical dysfuntionatin' family.

What people don't understand is that ALL families have their share of looneyness, and despite all them ooey gooey movies about big OLE happy families, real life's a whole different story. Everyone's nuts.

So, I got this case cause the old fella done upped and kicked in the bin. Yep, that's right. He tried callin one of his stray kids to bust him out, and tweren't no way that was gonna happen. The old fella? He went apeshit, he said to his son: "She tricked me, she stole my money."

Turns out the OLE fella tried stanglin' the old buzzard to get some kinda comeuppance.

That's how I got the case. The kid, who's pappy croaked, was concerned he might go to hell for not bustin' him out. He said when he called, that he was freaked on account he didn't have no emotional sense about things, and wanted to know if it was in violation of one of the Ten Commandments. It's either the fourth or fifth Commandment depending on which Bible you're lookin' at. Honor your father and mother. The fella got to thinkin' he'd fallen short. Me bein' an expert of sorts I'd reckon was the logical choice for him to ring me up.

Before we go any further, let me tell you about the Big Ten. They're engraved in stone, but they are subject to interpretation: Thou shalt not kill? Hellsfire, there's war ain't there? Thou shalt not steal, a person goes out and swipes some food to feed their family, hellsfire again, that ain't no transgression. Thou shalt not commit adultery, hellsfire one more time. Did you ever see the way some married folks bicker? Goin' back to Bible times it had to do with a fella spreadin' his sperms, so kids wouldn't grow up bastards and all. Then again history's filled with famous bastards. And there's lots of temptations for folks to get all juiced up with Satan's favorite services, porno, prostitutes, and penis stiffenin' pills. Yep, them old geezers pop a Viagra, and youth flows into `em. Their old wives don't hold a candle to some hot little mini-skirted vixen. So's you can see these

Commandments was really the origin of a whole civilization of experts called lawyers. Gettin' back to the fella who called:

I tried to console him, but he was right sure he'd go to hell, for not doin' but for nothin. He called me, and I said I'd give it a look see. I did add, that hell was pretty crowded with collsarn politicians, folks with bad credit scores, and the onslaught of insurance adjustors (Satan's been fancyin' those folks for some time ever since the mortgage industry went bust). This was a busy time for OLE Mister Mephistopheles, but the kid, actually a grown man, an educated one too, was sorta freaked out. I figured me and Trip'd check things out. What gave me a brain itch about this unsettled soul shuffle was, that there might be some hinky stuff goin' on. Unnecessary damnation, on account the wrong people went to the wrong place.

So, off we went on a soul excavation research and redemption mission. We were off to Cleveland, Ohio. Ain't never been there, but hear it's pretty crummy.

Handicapping Human Life
Trip's slant on what went down

Eustice, had indeed spoken with Raymond X, the estranged son, who was living in Los Angeles with his wife Lisa. He was a slender silver haired man who took a look over each shoulder every few seconds as if he was being followed. He could have been, but I doubted it. He was in his late forties give or take a few years, and by the cut of his clothes, a knit shirt with a little pony on it beneath a well fitting blue sports coat, gold and steel Rolex, wedding band on his left hand, and a pinky ring on the other. He looked like a comfortable young urban professional. He introduced himself as a doctor, but clarified that he was a dentist. He was quick to say he had two daughters, who'd be missing him, and his demeanor was edgy, bordering on drug induced paranoia. Who travels three thousand miles to meet total strangers to have a state of the human soul interview? Hell I'd have taken a handful of whatever I could find.

These interviews are not particularly well documented or described in any professional literature. They'd get an "A" for awkward however, in the hands of professionals. A gentleman's "C" is passing. Usually the self-described professionals, the ones who exist somewhere between tarot and palm readers, and crystal ball gazers, it's a snap. They can weasel charge card and pin numbers out of a "client" in a snap. That's not our scene. Eustice and I sat down with RX at the aptly named lounge: The Rock and Hard Place, which was twelve miles from the Cleveland Hopkins International Airport, and a few more miles from the famed Cleveland Rock and Roll Hall of Fame. We found a corner booth, and sat silently until the waitress arrived, and took our orders. "Coffee all around Seeney said:"That's all for now." She left and under a minute later was back with three cups and saucers, cream, sugar, and napkins, which she placed in front of us, and then smiled and said she'd check back to see if we needed anything else in a few minutes. Her name was embossed on a tag over her left breast, and read "Luanne" on it in white lettering. Luanne looked old, and tired, and in need of any tip she could muster. She smiled quickly revealing poor oral hygiene, that look trailer park folks have from too many years of living on the cheap. "Thank you ma'am," Eustice raised his cup in a toast of sorts, "we'll get back at you," then turned and began asking some probative questions to our new client.

"Is there any money involved here?"

"Excuse me?" RX said. He was stirring the cream he put in his coffee with a spoon stopped, screwed up his face, and looked at Eustice with something approximating rage. It must have been the bulging eyes. "Is this some kind of scam, you guys gypsies or something?"

"No, not a scam. We're not gypsies. You'll have to forgive my associate, he's direct, and likes to get to the bare bones. Sometimes he asks awkward questions to see how people respond. You can relax we don't want any money we're a charitable outfit." Wiley held up an open palm and waved it. "Be cool. What my associate meant was IF there was money involved in this?"

"No. Not for me. My siblings maybe." He shrugged his shoulders, raised his cup and took a sip.

"I'm just curious why you'd give me a holler?" Eustice said.

"I read your books." Raymond said.

"Oh so you're one of the thirty or so." I replied.

"Yeah, yeah. You guys know the details of the damned."

"So here we are you mizewell spill, and we'll see if we can help." Eustice said.

"My mother had my father institutionalized, and despite my suggestions, that he remain at home, she insisted."

"Was he sick?" Eustice asked.

"No, not at all. In fact for a ninety year old, he was in decent enough shape to drive, give or take a fender bender here or there."

"I still don't get why you would fly us here to pry into an old man's death unless you're just racked with guilt or somethin'." Eustice said.

"No, not at all. I probably could have helped him out of the facility, but my sister barred the way. I just need to know that he was comfortable before he died."

"What makes you think he wasn't." I asked. It was odd. If there was something funky I'd think the law would have gotten involved. That's why Eustice asked about loot. What's with your mother, is she living large?"

"That's the thing," the dentist said. "It's as if he never existed, and by my not showing up to help the old man out it seems like he was erased from humanity."

"Hoowee, sounds like someone's tampered with the eternal remebrification of life. And I reckon that there is a damnable offense. OLE Mister Mephistopheles has a hankerin' for folks who don't pay their due to the dead. Did they at least have a funeral, maybe some prayers?"

"Yeah, but here's the thing. I didn't show."

"So you think that you gotta make amends somehow, huh?" Eustice asked.

"Yeah, I guess I do." Raymond replied.

"Son, if you stop doin' all that root canal on everyone who comes to see you, and do some charity work, you'll be free from Satan's clutches."

"How did you know about all the root canals?"

"They don't call me the collsarn best handicapper of the human race for nothin'. And that diamond pinky ring was a dead give away."

"Thanks, Mr. Seeney. You too Dr. Wiley. Thank you both so much." He pulled off the pinky ring, dropped it in his cup, stood up, and called Luanne over. "There's something for you at the bottom of the cup, and it isn't coffee grounds. Merry Christmas, Happy Channukah, and have a good life."

Mission # 507-BW

Hey folks I was tryin' to get some work done, when my cup phone rattles.

"Hey," I said.

"Mr. Seeney?"

"Thass me ma'am." There was some gal on the line. It really was a line cause my cup phones are made outta paper cups and strings, that go from my office, the Soul Salvation Center, on the second floor of the building on down to the lobby. Yeah, yeah, it's a big deal some'd say, but I know different. No lectronics on account I know the dirty tricks Satan plays. Nope, nothin' electronical in the SSC because the forces of Satan are real slick regardin' snoopin' and hackin'. My associate, Doc Wiley, says I'm looney, but that's tough titties. I got me the *BEST,* state of the art, cup, cord, and forces of evil filters in the corporeal world. Oh yeah, back to my cup call-the person says:

"I need your help Mr. Seeney," the voice rattled the bottom of my paper cup, and sent vibratin' ripples on my ear drum.

"Well, ma'am, I'll come unlock the door," and put down the talkin' device. I wish Wiley was here, that's one of the things I pay him for. That's part of his penance for goin' off to Sin City, but we'll be gettin' back to that.

I head on toward the door to let the lady in (I think she's a lady), leave'n my comfy chair I headed on over to the door. When I get there what I see was kind of shockin'. It was like some big ole fist took a whomp at my gut, and pushed my innards in so hard they was gonna come out my nostrils. Hoowee, it was a gal of sorts, but it was more like a transgendrical. All one and a half head taller than me, big ole Adam's Apple in the neck, and shoulders so big across you could rest twenty bibles on `em. Collsarn muscles were bulgin' out of her (or his) dress like some weight lifter. A regular Arnolda Schwartzenwhatever. But listen up: Over here at the SSC we don't take to no bigotizin', bad thoughts, or negativeness. If someone finds us and needs their soul saved it is my sworn duty to help `em on up. I just hope I don't have to do anything with this person's privates. That'd be the Doc's job bein' an MD and all.

"Howdy ma'am, or whatever you want me to call you," I says as I start unlockin' the door.

"Hi." That was a voice so deep Nurse Sharks coulda been swimmin' there, feedin' off the sand and seagrass. It was a troubled voice, and I couldn't right tell if it was filled with remorse, sadness, or some hinky thing.

"C'mon up to the office," I says. The gal started to walk toward the elevator, and thank heaven I stopped her before she pushed the call button. "You can't do that!" I hollered.

"Why?"

"You don't know, you really don't?" I had to eddycate this person right here right now.

"We only use the stairs, on account elevators are Satan's special soul snatchin' zones. There's music that's piped in, you know that, right?"

"Yes, it's called Muzak."

"They want you to think that's what it is," I said. I had to take a share the knowledge moment, and stood there and explained in a not-too preachy tone the way things is:

"The minions of Satan have rigged every elevator with a direct pipeline from Hades. Sort of like Hanoi Hanna, Afghan Annie, or Tokyo Rose. The sounds you hear on an elevator are to the untrained ear the old time songs. Well, they're actually songs that are interlaced with specially engineered demonic suggestions. What they used to call subliminal messages. What happens is them sounds actually are brain worms bein' planted in your head, that intermingle with your regular thoughts, and you start to thinkin' evil thoughts. And the longer the elevator ride, hoowee. Uhn uh, we don't use no elevators. That's lesson number one for visitors. Plus, the doc will tell you, takin' the stairs is good for you. You understand that now? Brainworms, that's what Satan's minions try to plant in people's heads any way he can. Get it?"

"I think so." The person narrowed her/his eyes, and looked at me like I done had bugs in my pants, and said the word to herself in a whisper.

"Brainworms." And then shrugged.
"Don't go lookin' at me like a crazy man. I done been to hell....TWICE."

"I know, Mr. Seeney. That's why I'm here, I just wasn't prepared for all the information

When we got to the office she took a seat. I was a bit winded from explainin', but finally said: "What brings you here today?"

"Sundays." She said.

"What?"

"I need to know why they have to on Sunday instead of on Tuesdays."

"Sunday is the official day of church goin' folks. Just ask anyone."

"I have, but I'm here because I need to change this."

I ain't particularly in the racket of diggin' deep into the why or what somethin' somebody wants, so I said:

"Let me look into this."

TIME
Seeney's Swiss Movement

You look at a clock and there it is. The what o'clock sticks there just so long as it takes for it to budge on over to the next marker. Before you know it all the what o'clock's add up to a measurable period of time that's filled or empty. It all depends on who's looking at the measuring. You see, there can be a whole giant gap between one minute, and the next. Filled with all sorts of stuff, plenty of them with things outside your realm. Did cave dwellers have to go out and fetch one thing or another at a certain time? Did the antelope hunters on the Kalahari need to know what time it was to hit the plains? Nah, they had the internal rhythm of their bodies makin' those choices. So you gotta ask yourself, who invented "time?" We've come to take for granted that it needs to be measured. Was there an "Andy Appointment?" Maybe it was Tommy Rolex, Tim Timex, or Cassy Casio. Now if you reflect back to ancient times Cassandra, also known as Alexandra, was this Greek mythological gal who could predict the future, but nobody would believe her. She knew about the Trojan horse and all that mythological stuff, but nothing she said was taken seriously. So she was punished by the regional deities of the time. She was like a clock that always knew what the "real" time was, but nobody cared because they all had their own time.

So here we are, humans aging. No, we don't really notice it much when we're starting out, on account we're too busy with other stuff. Maybe youngens shouldn't have watches or clocks? But they do. They are either on their iThis or iThat, or on some cell phone or computer. They later find out, when a little worldliness kicks in, that they are being monitored. When they do figure out that their individuality isn't so individual, and they're just cogs in some giant machine, giving a shit isn't an option. Then there's the pre-ordained timing of how our bodies rot: apoptosis. That's a genetic pre programming of cell death. It's why dogs shed, or chemotherapy patients lose their hair. We rot. It's a human thing for us to grow stale, fester, and fall apart. That's time. That's the human experience of time passing, and the options aren't that terrific. There's booze, but that speeds up the whole process. Dope, same thing only it numbs the sense of things falling apart. That is what the passage of time and the human experience is. It's an escalation toward randomness. A series of changes leading to a grand scattering, that ultimately ends in our demise.

Most of the diseases we end with are diseases of randomness: cancer, heart disease, neurological degeneration, bone erosion and decay. In general it can be tinkered with from the womb on down the line. We begin as embryos, random cells that come together through ordinary means: fucking, and the cells divide. Mitosis, or cell division, goes on until we're about 19 or 20, and all the structures are formed. After 22 or so it's all down hill. Whatever we accrue by the time we're at the top of our form has to sustain us throughout the time we have left. So the o'clock's measure the o'shits, and the random dispersion of cells moving about goes on until that, which is universal to us all finally kicks in.

I'm just winding up for the pitch, so stay with me on this.

What if I were to say that measuring time is not only silly, but the more you measure it the faster the cells move. Hastening the wildly growing misguided (like I said we only grow until about age 22 or so, and then it's downhill) cells?

So I've been workin' on this notion, that since there is time, a measurable sun up to sun down, and every second in between paradigm. There must be an opposite paradigm where this can be reversed. Not only as a matter of perception, rather an actual reversal of the entropy, or randomness of the universe. The very nature of the universe functions on an ever expanding bag of marbles, that scatters endlessly through space and time until they're so far apart from each other in distance and moments that they're no longer recognizable as marbles. In a sense I'm a marble gatherer, and believe that you can apply the laws of physics, gravity, mass, momentum, and all that Tommy Rot some kid invented for us to study, and be tested on. Make the universe make sense for us long enough to pass a test, so we can move on to the next level of randomness. Those good memory cells, before their orbits decay, go to work doing things that allow us to put together enough junk-food, cars, homes, all the material stuff to last us when the real rot kicks in. Oh no, this isn't unique to this age or another. Nope not at all. Thingk about it like this:

Didn't Odysseus have to pass through the Pillars of Hercules? He sailed beyond the limits of the known world. Francis Bacon toyed with this in Dantes Inferno, and H.G. Wells marvelled over time travel, as well as countless others. All ran up against the same obstacle: Time travel, tampering with the essence of the species, quantum mechanics, cellular decay. Marginalized whimsy into tales of fantasy. They became outcasts, quacks, charlatans. In fact they were set apart from larger society as evil, Satanic, Devil worshippers. It was a bad gig to tamper with the way things worked. Still is.

So I'm a charlatan, pleased to meet your eyes. I can go between the moments, freeze them, and hold them together. The way someone who's gotta drop a deuce squeezes their butt cheeks(often unsuccessfully) to keep them from shitting their pants. Are you ready?

A NICK OF TIME

I hear that expression a lot. Never really gave it much thought. But iffen you get to thinkin' about it, time eeks by in ways that're kinda unique to each situation. Sometimes it can take forever for a few seconds to ooze by. Other times, a collsarn day zips on by like a blink of an eye. That Einstein fella (I met him in Hades, but that's a different story), called it relativity. Best I understand, that theory goes like this: You put you're hand on a hot stove, it feels like forever. You get to play goosey goosey with some hot gal, it ain't but for nary a mini moment. There it is in a nutshell-RELATIVITY.

Now gettin' back to gettin' a little piece of time for yourelf, maybe whittle it off some time space continuum clock. Keep it all sealed up in case you need some extra time someplace, that there is what I'd reckon to call a nick of time. Thanks to my dubious days down Hades way, I learnt that time don't mean nothin' after you're dead. Sometimes it can drag on in life years for centuries. But in Hell time ain't but a second. See I never told nobody I had me my good old Casio strapped to my corpse. But we ain't gotta tell nobody, right? So one day in Hell could be like a thousand years, dig on that one. Since I nary spent that long there I managed to catch a few slivers and tuck 'em away. I'll get to that later, and how them "Nick's in Times" come in handy.

In all honesty, I gotta tell you that sometimes I get to feel like I might be a little tetched in the the old thinker brain, and gotta question myself. But, I had this thing happen that reaffirmed my mission here on earth, so just bear with me okay?

You're guide,

Eustice

WHAT WOULD JESUS SAY ABOUT CARS?

*Hoowee I'll tell you right now how I found out
and got convinced I was on the right path:*

It was the middle of the day, I'd just got done at the grocery store, and was walkin on back to the Soul Salvation Center. Just like that I hear the roarin' of a car motor revvin' up, and comin' outta no place. There wasn't many cars on the road, and I had to take a double take on this. Coulda been a hallucination, or better yet, a vision. And just like that this happened: This bright red, I think they call it Fire Engine red, on account it looks like a fire truck, came rushin' on up the street so fast I had to jump outta the way. Dropped my collsarn bag of groceries. There weren't even no fires, at least I didn't smell smoke. Tarnation! That was one damnated sumbitch. I was cussin' out loud when the car whips around and pulls right on up to me. It screeched so loud I thought my ear drums was in the back of a symphony, and the conductor sprouted a boner and threw everyone off key.

"What the hell you doin'?" I yelled out.

This car was fancy as fancy can be. Ain't seen nothin' like it, never. Coulda been a Ferrari, Aston Martin, Lotus, Bentley, all rolled into one super duper sports car. Collsarn motor was idlin' so smooth that it sounded like a fast tallkin' slickster, whisperin' good deals on junk at me. I was gonna give the driver a real what for, and had my hands on my hips in the middle of the street, ready to sail into this menace to humankind. I think it mighta been a school zone too. I wound up for the pitch. Maybe I could save his soul too. Never know when a customer might appear, but I was ticked on account my groceries got spilt.

The door opens. Didn't make a creak, squeal, or nothin', and I see a foot touch the road. It's a sandal. Ain't got no socks on like them Europeans neither. The fella stands up, and he's got long hair and a beard like The Dude. He's got on some white robe and raises up his hand.

"Hello Eustice," he says, in this real ghostly voice that echoes.

I know this guy. I seen his picture since grade school, in bingo halls and stuff. But he's here, now, in the flesh. I also remember seein' him someplace else...maybe a dream, or a vision, or maybe, just maybe when I was in that afterlife thing. It's JC HIMSELF!

"Jesus Christ!" I holler, and don't right know what to do.

He waves me off like it's no big deal, and walks over to me. I reckon I must've been jaywalkin' or somethin'. He just stands in front of me and says:

"What do you think of the car?"

"It's right fine" I say, lookin' closer at it. It's some kind of hybrid. There's music playin' on the car's high falutin sound system. I can hear it, it's that oriental guy, Gangnam Style, blastin' away.

"What on earth?" I was thinkin' out loud. I shoulda knowed better that JC could read minds.

"I'm visiting." He said. Now the Saviors voice seemed to carry on a wind that came outta nowhere. In fact, just like that, there we were in the middle of nowhere. I right don't know how, but somehow, someway, we were transported like by magic, or some divine power, into an intersection in the middle of a great plain surrounded by farmland. Fields of corn, wheat, oat, and the sky goes all shimmery.

"What's goin' on Son of G-d?" I say. "I been doin' my job right ain't I?"

"Now, now, Eustice," he said.

"Really I'm workin' real hard at savin' souls. I just want a shot at redemption. Are you here to take me?"

"No no, that's not what I do. That's the work of the angel of death, and he's been very busy."

"So what're you doin' here Mr. Christ?"

"I stop in on humanity to see what man's accomplished in the corporeal world from time to time, and see what the best, man can do. The pinnacle of man's creation is always of interest to me and my father."

"What do you mean sir?"

"Well, Eustice, man was created in my Father's image, right?"

"Yep, I know that." I says.

"Well, the Creator of the Universe, creates. Man's primary duty is to be creative. Therefore, I come to see what man's created, how far he's come with the tools he was given by my Father." He pointed upward.

I gotta tell you the sky went all funny. Not funny ha ha, but the clouds they got to movin' around like a kaleidoscope, or prism or somethin', and I felt a warm and good sense like I done just took a hot bath .

"So you're test drivin' that car to see what us mortals are up to?" I asked.

JC looked over his shoulder at the vehicle. "Yes, Eustice. It's the very pinnacle of man's automotive abilities, the finest car human beings can make."

"And you're taking it for a test drive, right?"

"That's right." He said.

"What do you think King of Kings?" I had to ask.

"It's all right. I think it's a little stiff in third gear, but it's good. Man's doing fine."

"JC, I got me a question."

"Yes," he said.

"How come you ain't lookin' into all the bad stuff, you know, poverty, hunger, war, the man's inhumanity to man stuff?"

"Good question Eustice. That's man's job. My Dad wrote the rule book, and man has to follow them. His sole duty is to follow the rules, and to be creative. Man must be as was written, creative himself."

"Oh." I scratched my chin. "So you don't really answer prayers, or go heal the sick, stop fights, or feed the hungry, do you?"

"No, Eustice. 'That's man's' job. Man can only redeem himself by his deeds. Following the teachings of the Good Book, and refraining from man's inhumanity to man."

"Oh." I said, but didn't really understand. Here's JC on earth test driving a sports car. What the he....I caught myself, and had to ask another question. Why not, I had the fella right where he wanted me?"

"Please continue, Eustice"

"I got me this question," I said. "Am I doin' right by tryin' to save souls from damnation?"

He smiled at me and said: "We'll see Eustice, we'll see. He put a hand on my shoulder. I felt a jolt go through me like electricity, and it felt good. He turned got in the car, and without much ado raced the engine a few times, shifted into gear, and peeled out. I watched the car drive off toward the horizon till it reached the vanishing point, and then there was an audible "pop" and the world changed. I was back in town in the middle of the street where I started. My groceries on the ground, and somehow, it didn't matter. I knew then that whatever it was I was doin' was just A-OK, and that my mission of savin' souls was the right thing to do. Yep. I think I had what they call an epiphany, or somethin' like that.

Well I hightailed it back to the Center right quick. I had work to do. I had me one wild surprise waitin' on me when I got there. Didn't right matter, on account I was on a mission from high above.

SHE CUT OFF HIS JOHNSON!
But that's what he really wanted...

There was a big hootered gal in the waitin' room that I ushered on back to my thinkatorium. Bein' all charged up, I figured that I couldn't right talk to her with all my attention on meetin' up with the bosses son. I had some things needin' studyin' up on that we'll get to later. But there was somethin' off-kilter with this person. Real off. I knew I had to go learn about some things, and was gonna go talk to some priests, rabbis, and other folks and learn on up about the holidays we celebrate but big hooters sent me for a loop. I sensed she needin' soul salvation but there was somethin' more she needed. I couldn't right tell, but knew I'd find out. I wish I would've had more focus, but who does after meetin' the Lord?

I was preoccupied and had Doc Wiley do most of the listenin' while I was listenin'. Trip was busy nappin' so I woke him, and said to do what he could to get as much info as he could, and I'd ride shotgun in the interview. So much was swimmin' around in my head that the bad vibage barely put a dent in my glow left over from that meeting. Like everyone on earth, she had a soul, and for the most part if they're at all reasonable, no matter what they done, in most cases, it could be salvagable.

Let her tell her tale, I tole Doc Wiley. Let her tell it and get a recording so we could listen on up later. But after a few sentences somethin' struck me real serious. It was as if OLE Mister Mephistopheles made a play for us, and that meeting with the Lord wasn't coincidence. This here could've been a spy for Satan. I held my horses and I listened good, and what I heard made me wan to throw up over and over. But in the end, which I wouldn't find out for spell, just like the heading says...She done hacked it off, and it wasn't in just that metaphysical way. This mission was goin't to be complicated, and the big hootered gal, became in my thinker brain's eye, the mean hootered gal. This is what happened that day. Listen on up:

When she got to talkin' she seemed pretty straight forward. At first she seemed like another scorned woman and she wanted revenge. That was it, so simple, so pure and complete I reckoned this'd be a quick one, two, three, and she'd be set. But she went on, and that's when it got spooky. Spookier than the first time I got unconscious, and died on the operatin' table. Spooker than the fact that instead of seein' the bright white light, I saw a blurry, red goopy swarm of angy bugs, and they was draggin right on down to HELL. But that's another story.

Here's more of what the mean hootered gal telegraphed: Her idea of revenge was, at the first, I thought relatively easy. After all she was a scorned woman, on her way to Scorneo in hell, and she wanted redemption. She tole Trip that her "support group" of gal pals, superficial friends, and of course her adorin' mother, could do nothin' less than empower her. Trip tole me that her mother would even go so far as to donate real money for real mischief. She couldn't live with the torment that her husband would leave her. He had to be mad, on dope, drunk, or have some psychiatric illness. That sounds smart, believable, and her friends would buy into it, temporarily. She'd need some backin' on this. It could all backfire and her own motives become clear, as they had over the years, but not now. She had to get the penis off completely, and make sure those children were "taken care of" as only she knew best. That'd show `em all who's who. The broad wanted revenge and that's what she'd get. The money? Hell there'd never be enough. Especially for a gal approaching the wall. Thing is, she didn't see it coming even after she hit it. And she hit it hard. Her sagging tits hit first, followed about an hour later by her bulbous schnozz, and ten minutes later her forehead. If she fell on her ass it'd take her spine a week to feel it. She hated men, and all women were "sisters beneath the skin", not in any sexual way, because sex was somethin' you just did to get over with and then eat.

Judgin' by the curdles of cellulite on her arms, this gal liked to eat. And eat, eat, eat, I learned is what Tuffy loved most. There was a three day old taco on the desk she was eyeballin' and bein' the gent I am said: "Help yourself."

She did. I watched her wrap six fingers of one hand around the plate and not let go until she was done. I later learned she'd been eatin' like this since she was a kid. I learned from her lots of things I'd have rather not, but did. She said she had a prize from the Clean Plate Club. Some imaginary cheering section her mother set up to give her a pat on the back. One of many pats, because Tuffy, flattery operated as she was, needed constant praise and adoration to get anything done. She'd hold court in the bathroom surrounded by her pets. Two dogs, a cat, and a canary would listen to her fart, fizzle, and plop. A phone sat next to the crapper, that she'd use to call her mom to boast about the doody ball and hear: "Don't flush princess. I'll be right over and we'll get a picture of it." Yep this woman was not just bent, she was a pretzel with an M.C. Escher reflection in the

What in tarnation was wrong with this broad?

I get to thinkin' the poor sap didn't see it comin'. Nope the kid had just turned someteen or somethin' when she tied the twine `round his soul. Draggin' him from a waistband she called a belt, she said: You were born a woman in a man's body. And she took it from there. In my mind's ear I could hear her deep murmurry voice like an out of tune base guitar with the volume all amped up.

That was just the beginning. There was more to do with her life, another few kids, and a few million dollars to get to fucking with their heads. Hoowee-she WAS above the law. I didn't know for certain then, if she was one of Satan's helpers. But I did know for sure that somewhere, somehow I was gonna cross paths with Mizz Meanhooter, and it wasn't gonna be pretty.

She left the office that day and offered to pay us for the consultation. I told her there wasn't no fee, but she threw money at us and left, and then said we'd best not tell a soul about this, or else.

Trip and me looked at each other, and both of us shook our heads. This was trouble, and that woman, if that's really what she was, was gonna drag both of to the devil's door, and dump us if she could. I could see Trip was agitated, and maybe it'd be a good idea for him to take some time doin' worldly things. Maybe find a regular gal and do some carnal stuff. Maybe stop off at the grocers too on account we ws low on grub.

For now I'd file away them things, cause there was another case in the waitin' room. When I walked down the hallway I still smelled the foul stench of Mizz Meanhooter, and her johnson choppin' man hatin' ways. I still might've thrown up a few times, but I held it back. Hoowee. There's so many foul things of this earth it's a miracle human's survived as long as we have.

BILLIONSNESS
Evoked by the truly mad

It always seemed to surface at one time or another during the day. Like a rush a acid from stomach to mouth, and the bad taste didn't wash out of his mind. No, nothing dampened the disgust, despair, and drawn out murder of his son. No matter how many other thoughts, ideas, notions, concepts, or flights of fancy. The fact is, that the bitch set her sight and moved in for the kill.

But he wasn't quite dead, or maybe he didn't know it.

The fake genetic tests, the years of psychological chess, the absolute and complete conclusion that her revenge would make life somehow right, drove her into premature old-age. It drained the capital put away for a rainy day, but the kid was on gurney headed toward a new life. Oh he died that day, and she killed him. The cunt did everything she could to make sure no one would interfere with her chance to extract revenge. Even if it meant using her own son as the weapon.

ZANENNA TALK
The Language of Scorneo

Now as a point of reference I got to tell you this: When I was in hell there was a special compartment that was set real far off from the others, on account it wasn't just noise, but the sounds coming from it irritated even Satan himself. The Wailing Women of Scorneo.

Scorneo's that place in Hades where scorned women go. Ain't no two ways about it. They could've avoided goin' to hell iff they woulda got on with things after their dee vorce, but instead they opted on in to take full out life long revengefulness on their ex husbands. And because they went through so much emotional capital, bad juju, and negative vibage, that done spread awfulness to other folks. I think that mighta been a damnation point, I'm not so sure, but I'll get back to you on that.

The scorned women folk are worst when their husbands, or their ex husbands, marry on, and it's usually to someone younger and prettier. Well these scorned women get to a boil and go on and on every chance they can to trash their exes. They plot and plan, figure out ways to impede their lives, and pull the time honored trick of using the children as tools to accomplish their revengefulness. Yep, they use them kids as pawns. But the way the earth rules are, everyone's always talkin' about the children. For the children, the children's best interests, the best care for the children, children's needs, and on and on if you catch my drift. A rotten person could cash in on usin' children to advance their position in any situation, iffen they stick to the mantra: "It's for the children."

I don't reckon there's a person on the planet that wouldn't give `em some sympathy, and a smart gal could parlay that for years. Even if it really wasn't in a kid's best interest, a truly evil gal could fudge it good. Nobody would question a mother takin' care of her kids. Or would they?

It turns out that in the final analysis, women that turn the kids against their pappy for marryin' another gal or somethin', get what's comin' in the hereafter. On earth they usually see their friends drop off fast from all the blabberin' about how bad mens are. Yep, scorned women get to hatin' menfolk because they don't trust `em no more. That carries over on to the kids, and the kids develop a hate-on for their pappy for leavin' poor, poor, pitiful momma. That only lasts as long as she can keep up bein' theatrical-like, and keepin' folks convinced she's a victim. Yep, gal who's been divorced, no matter how much money, treasure, or beneifits she gets, bein' felt sorry for goes a long way. Heck, bein' a person in the hood is slick place to be. You can get a whole lot if you live there. That hood is victimhood, and hooweee, it's a real good way for the scorned to exist. But sooner or later it catches up. There's only so much sorry you can feel for someone, especially when you realize they're just milkin' it. It's when the kids get to growin' up and all the years go by, and mommas still playin' victimmy-Pitiful. But it really isn't. She usually ends up all shrivelled up, mean, and foul smellin'. I seen plenty of `em. They have a tendency to hang out together, and have their own language. They call it Zanenna Talk. The language of scorned women.

I had me a more than a few of em wantin' me to extract out some kind of revenge over at the Soul Salvation Center, but when I told `em about goin't to hell they'd go off on me like a collsarn giant mouse trap pert near snappin' my head off.

I reckon you can imagine a humonguous hall filled with wailing women cryin' fake tears, seekin' sympathy from the likes of their own kind. Screemin' and hollerin' in that horrible tone that came out like a bad heart valve amplified so loud you'd think you were at a rock concert. And friend, let me tell you this: Of all the compartments of hell I'd been near, Scorneo was the worst, and if I hear Zanenna bein' spoke...I hide.

EUSTICE WAKES UP

"I came to an awareness like the lights went on, and suddenly I was walkin' down some nice path in the forest. The sun was shinin' and the wind was warm and gentle. When I looked up at the top of the trees they was movin' real slight, and the only sounds I heard must've come from the wind tickling those treetops. It sounded like the seashore, like waves rushin' up and then slowly crawlin' back to be gulped up by the ocean. I was thinkin' about what sort of ocean would gulp some crap up and then leave junk on the shore. When just like that, there was a crack like a whip, and one big ole tree branch fell in front of me."

Eustice had been unconscious at the roadside after a hit and run incident, and left for roadkill.

ADAM AND EVE

So they're I am in the Garden of Eden. Adam and Eve they're goin' at it like bunnies, but rabbits they ain't been invented yet. That don't stop 'em from runnin' around, schtuppin' over and over again, all day and night long. I reckon that after a spell they got a little raw, you know, down there, and took a break. Not havin' TV, and sportin' games back then, exceptin' maybe watchin' dinosaur races, Adam wandered off to take a whizz. Sure enough Ole Mister Mephistopheles is there, and says: "Hey Adam, lets go have a few drinks, hit some tit bars, and hang out."

Now Eve's over in the cave makin' sandwiches, all innocent, not knowin' Lucifer is startin' his evil trickery, and when Adam comes into the cave to say: "Eve, I gotta go. Me and my pal Satan are headin' out for drinks." I think it was in English, after all the Good Book is written in that language, but I'll get back to that later.

Now Eve, not knowin' any better, on account back in those days the three things women knew about sex was, let's do it, go get me some food, and hush on up. That was before all the women's libertation, Planned Paraphenalia, and voting and stuff kicked in. She was just happy making Brontosaurus burgers. Adam gave her a kiss on the back, she didn't have no clothes on, and that ole Satan was given that nice little tush the eyeballin'. After all he's the collsarn devil, and that there is how humankind began its decline. Why? Well we'll get to that later.

DARKIES
So much for political correctness...

I ain't talkin' about all coloreds just the ones got their attitudes all pumped up, on account they got a Negro President. Here's the deal: I noticed that ever since there's been a colored guy as the boss of the US there's been a certain edge, that American Black people have. It's as if they own the place, even though some do, but that's beside the point. I saw this colored guy mowin' the lawn at this here development, and asked for instructions to the liquor store. This fella looked at me like I was the dumbest piece of dog Poop on the planet. So what if I was on someone's plantation, the fella just flipped me the bird and went on with his grass cuttin'. I go on over to the grocers, where there's a bunch of coloreds. In fact all the workers are doin' their jobs in that laxidasical way, but they got "attitude" like they own the place. Coloreds have been mentally migrated by some inty lexual uppityness, on account they got a the ultimate secret weapon against whitey. At first it was nifty to have the first president of the country's history bein' a darky, but ever since, you can't get a day's work out of any jigaboo in America. They not only got this entitlement thing goin' on, but I been aksed for money because of the whole slave thing.

That got me to thinkin. All them years ago those people livin' in Africa were doin' just fine huntin'

Antelopes, dancin' around the fire, piercing their lips ears and faces. No big deal, I seen the pictures in the National Geographical at the doctor's office. Them women didn't wear no shirts, and their big ole breastesses would just be out there in the jungle danglin' around. And the fellas, their johnson's was so big their loin cloth covers were barely big enough to cover `em. Maybe they only wanted to use the bare minimum of animal skin. But they was happy colored. I don't think they were called that till they, the darkies, came over to America, and went into the slave business.

So I got to figure: Why leave the mighty jungle? All the animals you can catch, nudey colored gals floppin' around, and not havin' to wear shoes! Hoowee, they had it made.

Now I figure the laziest coloreds are the ones that turned into slaves. Some slave catcher probably hired a translator who could talk junglese real good. They'd go around spreadin' stories to the tribes, that if they came along they'd all get color TVs, Cadillacs, Malt Liquor, and they'd pass out Kool cigarettes to boot.

Then clincher was that if they, the darkies, signed on, they'd NEVER have to go hunt them wild animals no more, there wouldn't be no lions and tigers to fight off-nope-it'd be easy peasy Japanesey. Juss sign up, and life would be a dream.

Now that there is evy dense that the American Negro is shifty, sneaky, and only in the US of A because they're waitin' on all them free things that was promised. Not even free KFC, Popeyes, or a sixer of Colt .45. Heck, the price of a carton of Kools is more than most coloreds make in a week.

So that brings me up to the now. Black President means all them treats are just around the corner. Since they didn't get all them things all those years ago, they built up a lotta hate for whitey, who did all kinds of mean things, and didn't even pay them for it.

I reckon they can tighten up their lips, shake their head, and look down on whitey now, and secretly say: "We got us one of ours in the White House, and you're gonna get what's comin' whitey."

And that there is why these are some real nasty political times in the US. The jigaboos want payback, and the whiteys are knowin' that the only coloreds here are the offspring of the dumb ones. So they're waitin' for coupons, and whitey is keepin' the notion they're dummies fixed in their heads-That there is why there's so much political divisiveness.

Thank you for invitin' me to lecture at your graduation from the colored college. Hey stop throwin' stuff...you asked me to speak.

D.D. CROSS

SPRINGTIME IN THE GARDEN OF
STUPID, STUBBORN & JUST PLAIN MEAN

And like every day before it the moon's still up there, but for some reason the big ole chalk thumbprint sets there. I can see it from my bed, and it's bright. I ought get up and shut the drapes, but then I mizewell go and pee, and by then it'll be up time. I don't right care for up time every day. Some days there's stuff to do that's just flat out crummy. But I can see my hands in the spring moonlight and they're lookin' all shiny, and hoowee my finger nails are glowin'! Now I don't mean no simple reflection or nothin' nope. They was flat out screamin' neonish blinkety blink like some collsarn hootchie bar. What the Sam Hill is goin' on? Did I touch somethin' neonical in my dreams and wake up with some serious fingertip cootie? Maybe I poked through another dimension in my dreams, the ones I'd already forgot about on account the light from my fingertips was gettin' brighter and brighter. I took a slug of ayche two zero that was next to my bed and got to think I was still sleepin' and that this was some dumb ole dream. So I got out of bed and went over to the bathroom and started rinsing off my hands, my fingertips just got brighter and brighter.

CRAZY WORLD

What a crazy world it's been lately. Koreans with rockets, Iranians with atom bombs, Afghanistan, Africa, Oil, the whole shebang under one atmosphere just heatin' up like an innertube in a hot pool of murky water. Humans have gone mad, and that's supposed to end in a few months.

Thass right, the end of the world. Accourding to the Native Mexicans-what a dopey ass word that is too-Injuns, that's what they was. Either Mayan or Incas, I don't right know for sure and that Witchpenia is too confusing to look-and even if I reckon that it tweren't, it'd be the same deal: the world is going to end in 2012. You hear all these newscasters that make a whole lotta money to prance on TV with their newsie information that's as fake as cousin Clem's English accent. I'll tell ya about Clem, here:

Clem's a con man, not a real good one either on account he couldn't pronounce or understand the meaining of his own name-the dummy calls himself Clam instead of Clem and then tells people he can turn anything into an oyster. He puts a marble in his mouth and spits out a fake pearl. Magic Clem and his spiritual transformative skills-yep, that's what he calls his con. I gotta say he did okey dokey with it up till some kid gave him some red hot jelly beans and he went apeshit. Persoally I think he knew that'd be big trouble on account them kids was just foolin' with him-After all, I gotta scratch my head wonderin' what the hail Clem was doin' tryin' to con kids in the first place. I'd have to reckon they was the kids of newscasters, and Clem was tryin' to get on TV so he could pitch his schtick to the world. Dummy.

Them news folks get paid millions and millions of good old `Merican TV stations to lie to dumb people who believe what they see on TV over and over again. This week it's about this colored kid who got hisself shot on account he had on a sweatshirt, and the news folks, who I personally think are propaganderin' people so they don't think about the real problems, like the war, the lack of insurance for sick people, the folks that ain't got no jobs, and the general mess the world's in. Yep, the news was invented by polly ticians who wanna keep people dumbed down and all hepped up about things that don't really matter in the overall scheme of things. Like who's gonna care about birth control if the world is gonna end in a few months?

Think about it-a gal get's impregenatized, she ain't gonna be here when it all comes to an end. `Cept I got this theory that the newscasters have some kind of rocket ship to save their newsy asses come the end of the world-whoosh `em away when gravity stops workin'. Good for them, they deserve each other floating around the heavens yacking fake stories to each other. So maybe old Clem tryin' to get on TV and turn marbles into pearls wasn't such a bad idea-I'd say he was tryin' to get to rub shoulders with some newstronauts and maybe get himself a seat on one of the rocket ships-But his plan was dumb, and them kids that gave him a hard red hot, spice candy shaped like a marble blew that for him. I think he busted a tooth, and puked up his breakfast beer, eggs, and pancakes on the newskids, and did end up with the newsfolks in the end. But it turned out in a crummy way because Clem was one of stories-they portrayed him as some kind of school yard freak that stole candy from kids. They put him in lock up over in England on account of that crummy fake accent. At least he got to see some of the world outside of `Merica before the world ends. I think he's gonna be in lock down till way after the end of human history.

PRAYERSURANCE
Another Jim Dandy idea...

I got me to thinkin' about `Merica and all the folks who ain't got no health insurance. There's a lot of `em, but is it up to me to do anything about it? I reckon that'd depend on politics, and iffen I was thinkin' Republican it'd be to hell with `em-let `em fend for themselves. Then if I was Demoncrat-let `em get on one of them exchanges that ain't supposed to happen cause that colored fella runnin' things, I mean that African American guy, well, wait a second his gramps or something was African African, so it's confusing...whatever-The thing is, there ain't no real regularness in healthcare for people livin' in the US of A.

If you got a condition, like the sugar, or the pressures, or some other pre existifyin' condition like pregnancy, you gotta pay an arm or a laig to get insurance. And if you get a arm or a leg chopped off you can't get it sewed back on iffen you ain't got no insurance. So wait a second, if you ain't got a job, and you got some problem, how do you get took care of? Some of them political folks say to pray. Praysurance. Sounds like a good health plan.

But then you got countries like Canada and England where everybody got insurance coverage and there's no bills and nobody asks if you already got a problem. That makes sense if you believe in bein' decent. Hoowee, I'm startin' to get to think that the US of A is becoming a very outlaw type of place. The whole country is just out for themselves all selfish and greedy. The more you got, the more you get. I guess in some way that'd sound just about right-sort of like pirate times.

Are them polly tishins just givin' `Mericans a bunch of bull pucky Praysurance and then they get all that fancy coverage?

Heck, you gotta either be real poor, or livin' large to keep livin' in the USA.

I'm beginnin' to believe that the worst enemy of the USA is the USA itself. Pitiful.

MEANDERINGS AT THE EDGE OF SPRING

Somewhere it's always spring, a new this, or a new that, a rebirth, reinvention, and a fresh start. The problem a lot of folks have is findin' where that somewhere is, and most of the time it's right there inside them all along.

Here's an interestin' fact, the human mortality rate is 100%.-Did you know that? No one leaves here. What are you goin' to do about it? Be miserable? Be satisfied with what you're doin', or what you have, or don't have? Remain a prisoner to the ailment, malady, or hideous deformity you've got? Lots of people-sure you've heard this all your life, have it much worse than you. The mere fact that you're readin' this is testament that you've still got a shot. But at what? Any age, any location on the continuum of a lifetime there's always goin' to be just this or that which isn't falling into place. Those gears, or tumblers aren't precisely in line, and that machine of life just isn't hummin' along just so. So? Is it supposed to?

I'm miserable, but I'm glad that I can feel a genuine miserable feeling today. Maybe I won't be tomorrow, or the next day. Maybe I'm exhilarated, one day, down the next. It's a carnival ride, and you make your choices about what ride you're going to take. Go on, have a cotton candy, some tafe or other treat, but don't lose sight of the possibility that you may break a tooth, or feel crummy later. But that doesn't matter now does it because you still aren't sure about what to do with yourself. Maybe you're in a rut, a bad marriage, a bad relationship, a bad job, crummy career, whatever it is-you KNOW, there's something more to this life.

Think about it, you can live for decades and decades, and then end up drooling and shitting yourself-living in memories that come in and out like fake spooks at the carnival ride tunnel of doom. Whoopee. Or you can nab the Escalade of doom, that instant heart attack that takes you out badabing. In the meantime, what is that one special thing you have the makes you get up out of bed and...nah, scrub that-too many folks don't even want to get out of bed these days, they're bummed out by this crazy world, which quite frankly hasn't gotten any less crazy with all the terror, and chaos, crummy economy, not getting what you want or need-simply surviving and the phone, if it's still connected ringing like made from the bill collectors dogging you like a herd of horny bulls.

Start this plan and you will feel just a little bit better. Not a miracle, but just a minor step toward. Some use towards, adding that s, but fugedaboutit, who needs an s when you can save it for a hit when it isn't? We'll get back to that. You wake up, don't really want to get out of bed. You feel like crap, but you've got some bodily functions to do-hopefully there won't be any blood or difficulty there, but if you've gone that far, and still feel like a turd-go back to bed for while. Stare at the ceiling-ten minutes later it gets old and the crumbly creaky thoughts ooze in, and things get dark, you drag yourself out of the sack and maybe you have some stimulant, tea, coffee, whatever, you may have a job, a responsibility to be someplace, but you still feel crummy, but you get on with it. You could take the day off and be a bum. Call in sick. Lie. Go buy a big sack of cheap high test beer and cigarettes, a lot of both. Sit down bright and early and drink the hell out of the day, watch daytime TV, smoking and drinking till you pass out. Drink the heart out of the day, suck up all those dopey shows. If you have a significant other they'll be pissed off, but you need to do this. You wake up from your stupor crack open another brew and chug it, light up another cigarette and keep going until the next time you pass out. You're hammered, stay off the phone.

Twelve or so hours may pass and that alarm clock will go off and you can't call in sick. But you really are this time. You have the shits, the headache of a lifetime, your mouth tastes like the bottom of a bird cage-a big bird's cage too-and you stink from the clothes you passed out in. Now deal with that you smelly hungover crumb.

This is how you deconstruct to reconstruct. Everything after this is an improvement.

There are people who do this every day for decades, they're called alcoholics, and they usually feel much worse than you, and die horribly. You don't need to do that. But at some point yesterday you may have had a glimmer, a glimpse of feeling damn good for maybe a minute or two...What was that?

Those were the dopamine receptors lighting up in your brain. The concoction of ethyl alcohol, specifically the nitrosamines in beer, nicotine in the cigarettes ignited them. They're not used to this sort of business, but they're there, and now you realize that much of that crumminess you feel has some biochemical basis.

Time to clear the deck, get in shape, and know some things that you don't-If you do what others have done, you'll max out your life, and feel better, you may even feel great, and enjoy every second you're alive. Skip the booze and smokes now, time for a few changes.

Oh yeah, if you have some medical problems and no health insurance. We're working on that-but hang in for a while, a fix is coming. I don't know when, but this IS America, right? So there must be a solution to the sorry state of healthcare in this land, right?

D.D. CROSS

AMERICAN CONUNDRUMS
Some things riddle but sure don't rhyme...

A free country where freedom is as an expensive way of paying for rights that are given away for nothing. Wait... The maddening nature of America's health care system will remain exactly as disarrayed as it has until it isn't. No one who is ill will be covered until everyone is well enough to be covered. The beneficiaries are, were, will be, and remain hidden. Lies, rumors, false hope, fraud and fuzzy farting creatures who sing songs and carry signs.

MESSAGE FROM A LIVING DEAD MAN

Howdy doody folks, it's me Eustice Seeney, and I got another doozie of a story to tell you. Are you up for it? Good, well listen up:

I been right with the world for a spell now and even though I got dead, went to hell, and came back on account some dummy doctor killed me from the bad anesthesia I ain't pissed. The malpractice money sort of smoothed that over. So I go around checkin' in on bad guys, and bad situations, and try and set them straight. Here's a few of them.

TIME AGAIN

Its movement or our movement within it remains a puzzle that'll probably never be solved. Say you travel back in time, would you remember the history of the future? I don't think so. Like if we we could go back to any point in history, would we be able to impact it or would it-the time period we entered-impact us? I think that once you reach a point in the past, everything you know about the future disappears. It goes away, poof, like the dreams you had the nigh before. Those neural pathways haven't been formed to have memories, because based on our senses to collect information, the snyaptic junctions haven't been formed, so that when you pass into the past, the junctions remain in your present. Then accrue again experientially as you function, in that period, so when you get to the present again, if you do, the memories of the past will be changed. So you can only change your won memories of the past when you get back to your own future.

D.D. CROSS

STAND YOUR GROUND AND SHOOT

Some kid got shot for being in the right place with the wrong pigmentation. Another guy in a war zone goes out and shoots people, gets charged for it, goes to jail. That's the news aside from a bunch of jokers running for office. Running for office (sigh)-they spend so much money that could be used to other ends, but out of vanity, idiocy, and plain old hatred insist, persist, and forge on in pissing away more and more to do less and less. Americans are disgusted with politicians. Radio talk show hosts blather nonsense and get people riled up. Riled up people drive cars, tailgate, yell, honk, and they get all road raged up. More people fight and shoot. Fight and shoot. Fight and shoot and hold your ground and call it self defense. Defend us all from the commercials that buzz in our ears supporting radio and TV yackers that incite nuttiness. TV and radio are beginning to evaporate as a means to get news because they only broadcast information the experts who make dopey commercials calculate what Americans watch. Everyone knows that nobody pays attention to commercials, or they click them off, change channels, and resent that commercials are on, and never buy the stuff they advertise. Fuck them, fuck the shooter enablers, phony news, and all the bullshit that comes over the airwaves to sell crummy products at inflated prices. Wastefulness perpetuates hatefulness, and panders to the inner sucker of every schmuck watching. Put ear muffs on your inner schmuck. Fuck TV and radio, unless it's an old movie without commercials.

DRUNK DOCTOR

Trip investigates an unwholesome vexing scene...

It has been nearly four months since the "drunky doctor," as Eustice refers to him, has followed up in any way. He has not called, written, or made any attempt to make things right with a client, who visited the Soul Salvation Center. The guy stated that he had concerns about this fellow, and that if nothing else he was going straight to hell. As a last ditch effort the client came to us for help. He described a doctor of sorts, someone Eutice had known, but was vague about that knowledge. Nonetheless, as an employee of Seeney I did my job, and investigated the man, and sought out data, which might result in the redemption and salvation of his soul. I'm still not sure what kind of doc he was, but he wasn't an MD. Here's how my initial consult with the client went:

"He grabbed my wife's ass, called me a hook nose Hebe, waved his gun around, and stumbled about his office in a dirty Spider Man T shirt. Maybe he is dead. Fuck that drunken bastard and Captain Morgan too. Douchebag. I tried turning him in to the AMA, but they never heard of him. He's going straight to hell. Straight to hell I tell you. But I want to see him pay some dues first."

I decided to look further into the situation and thus began case # 657.

I am waiting for the drunken doctor to finish his office notes. He has not sent them to the people that need them. He is a drunky man indeed. I know this because he is somewhat unrepentant, or willing to acknowledge that his consumption is not only hazardous to himelf, but others could be harmed. This may very well be why Eustice set out to "redeem" this man. He had his abdomen operated on due to anomalies caused by alcohol. Seeney said: "They was tore out and put back, all full up from booze," and Seeney believed the man was in jeopardy of eternal damnation. So here I am, scoping out the case. I visited with a pateint a few months back, and observed, as he conducted himself. It was a mess.

Despite his ills, sodden relations, and numerous DUI's he still kept it up. He defecates frequently, and has an aura of fecal aroma. I can understand why Eustice described this man as he did. Despite his obvious physcial decay, he still drinks until he passes out every day. He gets belligerent when he is drunk, and says mean things on the telephone to people. He called my wife a few times, and rambled on about nonsense. He called me many months ago when he was drunk, and told me he was a genius. Whoopee, I know a drunken genius who cannot figure out that he is a menace to society. I better not let him read this or he will shoot me and call it self defense. Bang bang. What an asshole drunk.

He had a few guns which he carried at all times. He bragged about how armed he was. Doctor Rectum aka Poop, kept one weapon, a tiny gat tucked beneath his white doctor's coat, and another strapped to his ankle.

He'd never hesitate to pull a gun on someone. Anyone he thought might be a threat real or imagined. My guess is most of the threats were imagined because of an alcohol induced haze, something that ran through his system twenty four hours a day. Sure he'd boast of how sober he was, which usually meant he was in the bag so often it was a miracle not to be passed out. But how much sobriety is left in twenty four hours if you start sipping rum at three or four in the afternoon, pass out, drink yourself back to sleep at midnight, and get up four hours later to drive to work. If you'd call butchering patients work. The slob never washed his hands, used dirty needles to draw up injections from the same vials, and called ethnic patients the rawest of raw names. He was a bitter quickdraw drunk with a streak of belligerence, so thick a 747 could land on it without a hitch. His patience runway was short though, and old Poop would draw his gun ready to empty a clip. Still he'd gotten away with it despite a few DUIs, a whole lot of lawsuits, arguments with everyone he knew, and dysfunctional with a capital D.

HOLIDAYS
A General Rap About Too Many Days Off

Hey folks it's me Eustice, and since most of you heathens don't pay much attention to the real facts behind these so-called special days other than the banks might be closed, or you ain't gonna get no mail. Me and Doc Wiley are gonna break `em down one by one as a mission to bring you the real facts behind the mythology and absense of those bills, that aren't showin' up on those days. Just so you remember, a bill, the first time it shows up, isn't really it's a bill, it's a notification that the real bill is comin'. So here we go. Either me or the Doc will go into the nuts and bolts, and what you gotta know to save you from eternal damnation. Are you ready?

Good. Let's get started...

New Year's Eve
This is when it all gets started...

Happy New Year from the Soul Salvation Centers! I'm goin' to get likkered up. Too much stuff was goin' and it was all on the TV. You probably saw it already, and it was bo-ring.

New Year's Day
They ought call this National Hangover Day

Hoowee I got me one hangunder. It's under on account it ain't over. It seems like last Sunday because the sun shone, water's wet, dogs bark and there's enough toilet paper to last until tomorrow. Here's a cool sentence: Shit. Shit shit shit shit shit. Shit. My haid hurts, and I feel crummy. I'll get back at you after them aspirin's kick in.

Twenty minutes later:

Much better. Where was I? Oh yeah, holidays, and celebratin' and stuff. You gotta conserve yourself `cause you could get real worn out from all the celebratin'. Most of it is observin' somethin' you can't see. So what I'm gonna do is illustrate the holidays of the year in an easy to understand way, so you don't use yourself up. I hope I don't have to use myself up altogether in 2012 `cause I celebrate them all.
Here goes:

The world is supposed to end this year according to some Mayan calendar. Yeah, right, like the world was goin' to end somehow twelve years ago on Y2K...a bunch of suckers spent a lot of loot makin' sure their precious stuff wouldn't get devoured by an absence of a digit. I'd have to reckon if a sniper lost a digit, as in his trigger finger that'd be a big whoop. Nobody lost a thing on Y2K and I doubt if the world is goin' to end in 2012.

I decided that I wasn't goin' to talk to anyone this year who made me feel crummy. So if any bill collectors are readin' this don't bother callin' because I won't respond. I'm not goin' to do a lot of things this year, but they're things I ordinarily wouldn't do anyway like: hang glidin', a trip to Nigeria, boxing a few rounds with Mike Tyson, or piss standin' up. I like to read in the bathroom, so this year I'm goin' to make it a point to catch up on even the most mundane of articles, ads, and glossy garbage that comes my way. Why? I'm really not sure. But somethin' about a clean hoop and a good read rings my happy zone.

Along the lines of happy zones-I've already touched on avoidin' assholes-of course I'd be considered by others to occupy that space-but, at this point in my life I can say fuck `em.

Last year I went through the roster of people who've been negative forces in my life and crossed off a slew of annoyin' folks. They were mostly people who'd expect me to drop whatever, and pay full attention to some nuanced thing or another they cared to chat about. Nope. No more needy assholes with bent agendas. I've got my own. Not really sure yet what my plans are for the new year, but they won't be includin' dickheads and will involve a lot of readin', and a lot of clean toilet seats.

VALENTINE'S DAY
This can be a bad trip if you miss it...

Hoowee you can get someone special right ticked off on account of missin' this holiday. I'd say it was Satan's tricky trap to get folks to buy roses, but don't want to spoil it. You see Satan, is also involved in dope smugglin'.

All them flowers get imported in big boxes, and they hide the dope underneath `em. This is the best excuse a fella can use. Just make up a nice card, and say nice stuff. This way you show that personal touch, and won't give money to them greetin' card companies either. They're also in cahoots with Ole Mister Mephistopheles. Yep those cards got Satanic messages in `em. You can show this to you're sweetie too iffen she don't believe you, or calls you a cheapskate. Some guys go out and buy jewelry and stuff, I don't know from that unless it's from one of the devil's outlet centers, and frankly the whole jewelry market's right well policed by the Hebrews, and they don't take but for nothin' when it comes to any of Satan's scummy ways.

St. Patrick's Day
EUSTICE

Like farts in a Mexican restaurant, time utters out and passes by. This year's been quick, I mean real fast. Just yesterday, in my mind's eye, it was Christmas time and now, St. Patrick's day is just around the corner. St. Patrick's Day is for some folk this: A Licensed to get drunk and act dumb. Not necessarily a celebration of religion as it is the spirits. but an excuse to drink and romp. Whoopee. Another day to keep off the highways, avoid sloshed phone calls, and other slip and fallery that comes a long with pewter livered revelers. My guess it the tribute to Ireland will leave a lot of hungover people tomorrow. Bleah. Don't drive, and leave me alone. Hang on a second before I start tellin' you about holidays...

I gotta tell you this, and it's important on account too many folks don't get it: When you live in a real nice climate, you know, warm all year round, Folks get to thinkin' everyday's a holiday...It ain't.

You can expect those unexpected phone calls from people you haven't heard from in years saying: "Hi, I'm in town, let's have lunch and drinks and go to the beach."

You scratch your head and say to yourself that you knew people could be stupid but just how fucking ridiculously ignorant can they be. Just because you're home happens to be in a desirable location, say, Florida in February, people, who you are acquainted with will pop in, on their vacation and expect you to drop whatever it is you're doing or not doing. Why? Nobody really knows but I've got a few theories beside this one: I call this the, just because I'm here concept. It's based on the premise of false presence. It goes like this-there's this dumbass notion that people from cold climes believe that since you live in the tropics you too are just sunning yourself at the pool, sipping Pina Coladas, and revved up to be available as a tour guide down memory lane at any time of day.

There should be some signal or poster at the airport or highway leading into some towns that says: Don't bug the residents-they'll call you. But there ain't.

So here's a poem you can send folks to sort of telegraph a message of sorts, or steer 'em away if you got to. The person who made me up, and everything else in this book done written it:

NOT DOING

Just because you're not doing anything
Anything at all
Doesn't mean you can drop what ever you're not doing
Just because they call

~DD Cross

That poem has a way of sucker punchin' moochers too. Wards `em off like BO keeps folks from waitin' on ya at a restaurant or store.

THEN THERE'S EASTER
Trip Wiley

So it's Easter Sunday today and the world is suddenly reborn-yeah, right. Same crap, different day, crummy newspapers, crud reruns on TV, and more of the same nastiness, which is epidemic in America in the 21st century. Please, I need a barf bag.

Have a foil wrapped chocolate egg. Better yet, chow down on some Matzoh..now you're talking-Hebrew soul food. That's right baby, spread a schmear of cream cheese, some butter, a jam or jelly and kiss goodbye to the tooth rotting chocolate bunny rabbits. You see Easter Sunday was never meant to be a religious occasion, no, not at all. The so-called holiday was developed by the secret world of dentists...that's right, you catch my drift. Rat bastard dentists. Fuck `em.

MEMORIAL DAY
EUSCITCE

This is a serious sorta day on account all them folks went off in the service and made a sacrafice. It's solemn, not festive, and people just don't get that fact. Seems like the post office shuts down, people have picnics, and beer gets drunk without much though to all them soldiers fightin' in all those wars. Right now, this very second there's some soldiers on watch, fighting, eating crummy food, and guys havin' a rougher time than you, me, or anyone here in the US of A sippin' brew, eatin' dogs, and not givin't these folks the props.

So I gotta asky myself what do you say to people? Sure's shootin' ain't; "Happy Memorial Day" but there are some dummies who do say that.

I'm gonna pass on fussin', speechifyin', or ramblin' about the seriousness of this day. It's a crummy thing more Americans don't treat the people in the barracks, on the ships, in the air, and on the battlefields with enough respect.

That'll be all for that, just don't forget our soldiers. That'd be just what Mister Mephistopeles'd cherish-let the bad guys in, and wake up one day lookin' into a big dark hole's what'd happen. Yep, if it wasn't for our soldiers some day we might wake up with a gun pointed in our eye, and someone jibber jabberin' some foreign language sayin' things in a not too fuzzy wuzzy way. Collsarnit, we might not even wake up at all!

JEWISH HOLDIAYS
EUSTICE

There's lots of `em. Start off the year in the Hebrew calender in the fall. Rosh Hashanah, the first of the High Holy Days that lead up to the big one Yom Kipur, the day of atonement. That's the holiest day of the year for Jewish people, and they're not supposed to eat or drink anything all day. They have to go and pray. Chant these things in Hebrew, and stand around all these smelly people. I don't think they're allowed to bathe or brush their teeth or nothin'. The New Year's Day, Rosh Hashanah starts off ten days when Jews have to reflect on themselves and the things that may have slipped into the sinnin' zone. Yep. Jews go to hell.

I reckon a lot of folks don't know it but back in Biblical Times there was a place called Gehenna. It's spelled all sorts of ways, and described in the Good Book, but I ain't goin' back to Sunday School teachin's. In them days Gehenna was Hebrew Hades. In reality, as man familiar with ALL THINGS HADES, I can tell you this: Gehenna was a garbage dump the old time Romans used to toss everything into, even Jewish folks, and stories got made up, and they got writ in the Good Book that JC went there and there was this big to do, and you can look it up on the computer on account this ain't a history book. Jews go to hell but sometimes only for a week or two. , They get to fess up to their sinnin' diffeernt from others. So you don't wish Jews a Happy Yom Kippur like you don't wish people a Happy Memorial Day. Both are serious times of reflection. Phew that was a tough one.

Then there's Channukah, Hannukah, or however you spell or pronouce it. It's a holiday that celebrates a lamp that kept burnin' will this fella Judah Maccabee went off to fight some people tryin' to kill Jews. I think it was the Greeks and the Syrians all those years ago, and it took a week. The lamp had just enough oil to keep the Temple lit, and the Jews managed to not get wiped out. Usually this comes around the same time as Christmas. I mentioned it here on account it's not as high, holy, or sacred to Hebrews in that cosmic observance sort of way.

Then there's Purim. That Holiday is about this King and Queen, and a bad guy who was hanging Jews on posts. The bad guy's name was Hamen, and the hero was a gal named Esther. The Good Book calls it-the story that is-The Book of Esther. This Hamen fella wanted to, you know, the usual, kill all the Jews...Well that didn't work out and there's a festive holiday for that called Purim. You CAN wish Jewish people a Happy Purim and they won't be offended, or cattywomp you.

Then there's Passover. That celebrates the Jews getting Exodused from Egypt where they were slaves. Yep, the Jews done built the pyramids over there. Moses was the son of Jewish folks, and they didn't want him to grow up a slave. His ma put him in a basket and floated him down a river, the Nile River where he was found by one of the servants of the Egyptian Pharaoh. He grew up to be a big shot in the Egyptian army but wasn't too keen on the gig. He had a vision, and set out to free the Jews. It took a spell but he talked to JCs pop, got some super powers, and sure enough led all the Jews out of Egypt into the Promised Land. They did have to wander aound the desert for a while, and Moses DID bring them the actual word of the Big Guy by way of two stone tablets. Those two tablets contained the big ten. That's right, the TEN COMMANDMENTS. The Jewish poeple built this arc out of gold and all this fancy stuff, and stashed it in there until Indiana Jones found it. But it's a festive holiday too.

There's a bunch more Jewish Holidays, and most of them, as you've seen have to do with not getting knocked off. So it'd be safe to say the Jews got some power lookin' after `em, they win more Nobel Prizes, have the best doctors, scientists, and lawyers, and make the most contributions to the world by way of art and literature by proportion to any other group. Somethin' like a handful of Jewish humans in all humanity compared to all the others. And folks really got a hate-on for Jews too. Maybe they think they're CHOSEN or somethin'-Personally I think they're collsarn lucky.

FOURTH OF JULY
EUSTICE

This here is America's Birthday, and cause to celebrate. Folks forget too often that the US of A with all its troubles and squabbles is the free world's example of a place where you can do what you want and maybe score big time. America's a business, and sometimes the business ain't so good. But you have this real good thing called the Constitution. The Bill of Rights lets folks like me speak my mind, and keeps cops from just tossin' me in the slammer without due process. Cops can't search and seize stuff without probably cause-I say probably because the cops pull you over, they'll probably find some reason to search you-but you got recourse if they foul up. That's why there's lawyers, Jewish ones.

I'll revisit this whole American notion again. But remember, despite all the flaws some folks say are in the US, the basic foundation of the country, the Constitution, is irrefutably the finest piece of gettin' your day in court document ever written. Hell you can sue anyone for anything and they can sue you. And you and me? We got rights if we're `Mericans. Yay, I tell you, I am real pleased to be an American.

LABOR DAY
Eustice never shuts up...

I don't really take a hankerin' to this one becaue I don't really believe in labor outside of savin' souls.

THANKSGIVING
Trip and Eustice discuss the occasion...

Next year. That's how I work it. I try to avoid my dysfunctional family at all costs. So I'll pass on that. Maybe Eustice will give you his slant on the Holiday's Hisotry.

"Hell's fire Doc," There he is.

"Don't you know that this isn't a real holdiay?"

"Shut up Eustice, it's a day to give thanks, and I'd be grateful if you let me eat some turkey."

HALLOWEEN

This here's a funny holiday in that it's cute for kids to go out and get candy, but some folks say it's evil, alomost Satanic. I don't reckon it is because there's so much candy bein' tossed around. Ole Mister Mephistopeles, who I personally know hates dentists wouldn't show up but for nothin' if there was Snickers Bars, Kit Kats, or Hershey Bars...NO WAY. So you can take the myth that this is anything but a kiddy day to dress up in costumes and toss it on Defenestrateion Day, which I will get to later.

XMAS CHRSITMAS, CHANNUKAH, KWANZA, WHATEVER

Before I get started I want to clear somethin' up: In Greek, the letter "chi" is written as an X, and in the old days when they didn't have a lot of words, they used a X for Chistmas. That there is all right, and you won't go to hell if you use Xmas instead of Chistmas on your greetin' cards.

This batch of holidays is mah favorite. I think I got the Hannukah confused with some other Jewish Holiday about some lamp and a war, but all those Jewish Days is alike in that they just celebrate not gettin' rubbed out. But Christmas? Hellsfire, we all know what that is, and the Good Book says we ought pay homage to JC. I reckon that they ought have called Chistrmas another name like Father and Sonmass, but since I didn't have no say in the matter, it is what it is. Stay out of the malls and keep some good cheer, and reflection on stuff that's private. Oh yeah, give things to charity anonymously because someone, and I mean the guy upstairs knows, and you get a few extra points added to your cosmic credit score.

DEFENENSTRATION DAY

That there is the act of throwin' someone out the window. It started back in 1602 in Prague Czechozlovakia some famous guy got tossed. Big whoop the last thing that went though that fellas mind must've been the ground. So much for gettin' famous that way. <u>De</u>, comes from the Latin meaning somethin' I don't right know, and <u>fenestra</u> is Latin for window. Maybe defenestra is like a siesta by the window, but defenestration is tossin' someone out a window. I reckon tossin' someone out a window ought be some sort of Holiday too.

The Unrepentent Drunk Doctor

Trip's observations, and discovery of a man in need of redemption...Case #DTriple9PooP

As part of my duties as a Soul Salvation employee I had to take meetings with some less than palatble people. One fellow in particular was compelling, and I thought that if anyone needed a soul saved it was this obdurate child in a man's body-an old, decrepit one at that. Listen:

I will call him Poop because that's the first impression that tickles your nostrils upon a first encounter. That fecal unflushed toilet smell, and booze, lot's of it. The request for his consultation was on my desk sent anonymously as most were, and one of us was to meet him at an upscale restaurant. Sin e Eustice, and upscale don't mesh, it was my gig. I headed out, and went over to the restaurnat on one sunny day, and greeted the hostess, an attractive young woman, who cluthed a stack of menus tightly over her chest, and notched her chin in the man's genral direction. Her eyes were watering, and after aprroaching I could smell the vapor trail and could see why. There he was.

He sits at the booth in the front of the restaurant alone, waiting for the other guests to arrive. Doctor Bigshot. He's a real wheeler and dealer. He can put deals together and, by his own description, is a mover and shaker of cutting edge practice protocols. Yesiree, he's a genius, or so he refers to himself. Not always though-he's got to be lit. Seriously hammered, as in Captain Morgan times ten, plus a few bottles of wine.

I Never thought a human being could consume that much alcohol and live. This guy did, and he lived...badly. Neglect, not just in his personal appearance-teeth in the sort of disrepair a beat up twenty year old Monza whose battery died during the Reagan era, and used as a planter at a trailer park with all sorts of weeds sprouting out it's cracks, crevices, and rusted out panels and flanks. Flossing couldn't help the old Monza, nor Poop's teeth. He had that jene sais quoi of someone who didn't give a shit, but; really did. He was fully flattery operated and made of point of reminding you, your friends and neighbors, or anyone who'd stand him long enough how smart he was. That was after he'd tear out his lexicon of ethnic and racial epithets to remind black folks of their Negrority, Italians of their Guineaness, Jews of their hooknosedness, and morphological stature as some sort of cute-only to himself-reminder of flaws in someone's character. Yes, poop was a genuine asshole.

This fellow truly did not have any redemptive qualities. This was a hands-on case for Eustice. Maybe he could pour him a shot; a shot of redemption.

I will run this by Seeney soon, and hand it off to him.

Another Wiley Day

I awoke today to the sound of rain ratatatting on the roof. For a few moments it was soothing, then another sound shattered the calming choir.

My muscles clenched hard when a bang at the door echoed through the house. Big house, old house, tired, cold, and cobwebby. The place had stood there for nearly a half century gathering dust, unpaid bills, and dangling chandeliers whose lights never shone on a Happy Meal, laundered with Cheer, or washed a dish cleansed with Joy soap. This was an unhappy home for the homeless that everyone who'd lived in moved out, leaving me to tend to the ghosts. Which I did just fine because I didn't believe in them nor them, I. Besides the rent was just right. Eustice picked up the tab-he didn't mention the palce was supposed to be haunted, just the right price.

The banging on the huge brass lion door knocker rate ramped up until it sounded like the crazed heart of a horse in heat whose chest was girdled with a wooden corset. I gathered the blankets and pulled my full bladdered husk of a body out of the sack, tripped over last night's pizza box and beer cans, and strode barefooted down the hall toward the staircase and stood there taking in the must, mire and, myriad mirthless moments spent greeting guests at the grand foyer. A place where once stood frolicking moochers, miserable guests and hideous haridans, all waiting for a hand out, free meal, a chance to rub elbows or pitch some half-baked scheme in search of coin. Creeps. That's who Eustice said used live here.

I thought about pulling on a pair of jeans and some shoes, but if I'd go that far maybe I'd hit the can first too before looking into the face of whoever was on the other side of the door. And there it was again, a syncopated series of soulless sounds stemming from the practiced arm of a pro.

How'd I know? Friends in need knock on doors with some hesitation, maybe a tap tap tap then pause and wait then another series of taps. Friends indeed just let themselves in. But whoever was here was not a friend or ex lover, no-a stranger, possibly some tenacious messenger carrying foul news, or some serious quatrain or summons, neither of which I'd care to deal with-so I hid and waited and hoped they'd just go away. I relieved my bladder and returned to bed, placing a pillow over my head.

The knocks went on for who knew how long but with each volley I heard a song. An odd discychony of rotten rhythms. Something was off in my mind. I wasn't processing things the wayI usually did, if or when I ever did in any right or efficient manner. Not in the eyes of others, my way of thinking that is, but unquely my own, an oddity not of volition but it was what it was. I really felt off at the moment.

I thought I'd awoken with a condition, an illness, some malady-I just didn't feel right in my own skin. What the fuck?

Despite the riveting nuisance at the door I had to know if I'd left my dreams and became awake with remnants of my minds debris-dream crumbs. Could that be it? Maybe my dreams didn't go away-I was stuck in one dreamscape or another. Maybe I was not fully awake at all, rather a place my mind took me to, and held me-stuck to me like a bad penny on a gum laced sole.

Oddness crept like the smell of staleness saturates the flesh of fools, fiends, psychopaths and funk. I stood in front of the bathroom mirror and stared at something I didn't go to bed as.

I put my hand up to the mirror and pressed at it with the tip of my finger. With a jolt I withdrew, this couldn't be real. My finger passed through the glass with the ease of moving from one space to another unimpeded by its density or that it was just impossible in any reality I'd ever known. There was some violation of the laws of physics and nature and fear should have been what came to mind-But no. This was something so profound I had to find out how much more than my finger could pass. So I stepped forward and placed my hand, at first slowly than up to my shoulder, gradually the fact that I needed to see-I had to see-what was on the other side. Where could it possibly go?

I knew it then that it was a dream, and the knocking on the door was just part of it-So my mind's eye saw that I was still in a dream and a mirror I could stick myself into was an invitation, somewhat symbolic yet part of the unreal reality that exists solely in our dreams, or so I rationalized. The banging on the door throttled up, but is shouldn't have. Maybe it was a heavy boot kicking at the door of my mind, kicking it down that made me climb up on the counter and with nothing to loose but to be awoken I passed through the mirror.

Mabye that's when I knew, an Epiphany of sorts, a crystallization that something was astir. Something more grand, more encompassing than the "Missions" Eustice had me involved with.

There was a shift in the balance of the world. As if the earth's axis had gone off-kilter, so did I, and whatever it was that drew me into Eustice's scheme could very well fortell my demise. I had to tread with care, maybe get out while I still had what I did, my sanity, and that was fading fast.

FUNKY DENTIST
Just another person looking for salvation

On Friday, February 3, of that year, Simon L. Bekirky, suffering with discomfort at the right lower jaw scheduled an appointment with his dentist with a reasonable expectation that his maxilofacial   issues would be resolved post haste. Dr. Alan Gershwitz, D.D.S. was having a relatively slow day, and according to his receptionist, Luanne Rheino he was, indeed bored, for lack of any patient flow at his office. In fact the only patient that day for Dr. Gershwitz was a fifty nine year old Caucasian male named Hans Bruger, not to be confused with the Hans whose fate was sealed in the feature Die Hard several years earlier. Hans, was quite alive, and having his teeth whitened had been a decade long goal, and Dr. Gershwitz was nearly finished with the very public, extremely vivacious male exotic dancer, who, had been told by his employer, Lenny Dake to brighten his smile or he would no longer be welcome to work the stripper pole at the female only-although there were a few homosexual males who'd snuck in-unless he brightened his public smile. A smile as mirthless and artificial as a smile can get. But according to Dake, male strippers nearing middle age who don't have appealing smiles, are worthless. The fact that Luane Rheino, while on a particularly long break, overheard the conversation and acted. She inserted herself into the coloquy and suggested to Hans Bruger pay a visit to Dr. Gershwitz, which he did last week. The dentist began the whitening process on the male stripper's teeth, and on that February morning he presented to the office for completion of the project.

So what was this about? Fuggedaboutit. He was concerned with eternal damnation and Eustice and me looked at each other, shook our head, and told him to leave.

BROADS: Finicky after forty? Wait until fifty...
Eustice

Let's face it women age crummier than men. They get more sag and drag, crotchety and mean, and just lose their damn looks. Ninety percent of sex, for dudes, is visual, and a good lookin' woman is imperative to initiation, countdown, and blast off.

Some skank snuggles into the sack and disrobes beneath the covers that there is hidin' some major prunage. No matter how much boner medication the guy takes you got a billiard match where the dude's usin' a strand of rope to hit the cue ball. Yep, the old marshmallow in the piggy bank. So I got this theory. Here goes:

You're a guy, maybe in your late thirties, maybe late forties, even fifties, or sixties and enjoy lookin' at women. Unless of course you're a homeo, and that's a different book I ain't been writ into. So these fellas, all of `em get curious about how gals age. Yep a dude likes to look. For instance a fella goes and looks up pictures of gals he knew way back when, and wants to see what the dame looks like. It's natural ladies, he ain't lookin' to step out on you, and sure's hell doesn't need a relationship.

This is to the women readin' this note:

I already said this was written to your man, so you are already a suspicious bitch and wanna know what you're man is up to and figure he's got messages from a bro like this all hid a way, or a love letter form some ho. Hey lady back off I ain't no bitch! I'm a bro, and this is man talk, so either clutch your gut, take a chill pill, or don't read your man's shit. OK? Where was I...Oh yeah, how bitches age...

Ever notice how gals like to go out of their way to point out some movie star, or model who's over hill and say: "Look at her, look how good she looks," and then turn their talkin' to their man in that "as if it was them" tone, and say: "See," in that self-righteous, justificated' to eat that next candy bar way that they's just as whatever the celebrity is?

Think Kathleen Turner, Sally Struthers, and Jamie Lee Curtiss. It's an awkward situation on account a fella's dumb outa words to say. Unless of coursse he's with one of them famous gals, and I doubt if he was he'd be readin' this right now. He might be eatin' some of that doody yogurt though.

Take a look at that Superbowel singer, Madonna, she was prime ass a few years back. All the women would say: Woo woo she speaks for all women look at her look at how well she aged, right? Of course she aged well, she got plenty of loot-you got fifty mill, you're gal would look pretty good at seventy too, but then we get back to the old aging deal again, and how women don't age. It ain't too well, is it? Then again some fellas look like crap all their lives. That's a different story. I'll get to that on account some of these guys are goin't straight to hell.

CASE #DTriple9PooP
Drunks Have Shots, But Few Got a Shot at Redemption

MAKIN' AMENDS

Some folks don't even bother makin' amends for things they've done. Maybe they don't know, or care, and if they did are just too scared of the consequences of fessin' up and takin' their licks like they ough. It can be a crummy life for a drunk who buries himself in that blackness of booze. Some famous writer, I don't know who it was, once writ that drinkin' is like lovin' and sex:

The first drink's like a kiss, the second, a few buttons undone, after the third-nekkid, come four and five? All bets are off. Finally a dark spot, a cloud maybe fills up your brain, and you get to stumble and pass out. When you wake up you don't remember but a thing. If you're lucky and your're wife ain't left you yet, you ask what you had for dinner-if anything at all-or who you called or what you said.

Drunky life is a hard life and you puke and poop a lot. When you wake up with booze the day's already shot, and that one day stretches into a week then a month and next thing you know you forgot what it was like not bein' so fucked up. Drunks is always tryin' to kid themselves sayin' theys cuttin' back or drinkin' less and not drinkin' the hard stuff but we know you're just bullshittin' on account that's what drunky people do. Bullshit. Never trust a drunk. Sooner or later and usually it's later drunks got to stop drinkin' because they'll croak. I don't like drunks, they are liars and sneaks. I don't suggest anyone deal with `em at all.

Dummies *Can't be* Changed.

Some folks ain't never alone on account their past is never far behind. No matter what they do in life, things got a way of catchin' up. Either in a memory that lingered beyond it's expiration date, or a wound that didn't right heal correctly.

We all see the same, but from different points of view.

So listen up and settle in cause if you're lookin' for a teaspoon of redemption it ain't gonna come from harpin' on things that ain't never gonna change. Among them things is thoughts folks harbor, store, and keep locked up in their heads. They hold them images of how you was or what you did and all you've left as a tool to keep their mind's motor runnin' in case they pass your way again. Iffen it's some crummy stuff you're liable to fall prey to a badness most folks have and carry for a long time. Shoot, sometimes they carry them thoughts on up till they die.

Some say that if you set out on a path of revenge you ought dig two graves. Maybe that's right, but it don't got no bearing on account we's all gonna be dead, and what happens then's been up for debate since humans started thinkin'.

Alls we got is now, not tomorrow-that ain't got here. Yesterday, that was in the past. But memories and thoughts? Hoowee, some stick with a person like bad chewin' gum on their soles throughout a cross country hike. And it's all just a hike, ain't it?

Yippie ki yay some folks like to say, but not me. Not no more. I know what it's like tryin' to remedy the past with words, gifts, actions-heck, you name it. Once you done been imprinted in someone's haid that's it-and that lasts as long as their forever is.

I don't quite know if some folks is just dumb in that way, or if some part ot `em got damaged deep down in their thinker brain in ways that can't be changed, tweaked or modified-But for some, once them cells line up in their heads, it's like a lightning bolt that don't stop jumpin' between clouds of thought. And thoughts is like clouds too-some of `em dark and fluffy, ripe for rain, others wispy scraggles that seem like they'd just fall apart.

Clouds may blow past and move away, or go someplace else in the world that's someone's head. But the cacklin' snap of neurons don't take nary a spark to move `em all together and get to stormin' fierce. All it takes is somethin' small to strike up the band and just like that, there's nothin' to rehearse-all them memories come shootin' back like they was never hid at all.

Yep time makes things fade away, some say evaporate, but lots of folks have said to me that though it ain't so great. The years roll by, life moves along, and other things occur, but all it takes is somethin' small, a sound a smell or word and somethin' happened years ago comes back like buffalo freaked out by ranchers with lassos ropin' `em in roundin' `em up makin' yesterday's madness be as strong as ever was.

So if you plan on mendin' fences, patchin' things up or swappin' words with someone who's got fixed in their haid you crossed `em, buckle up-Brains ain't made for openin' and I reckon that's why they call some hard headed. Notions don't go away-nope. They set and fester. Sometimes for years.

Sort of like a pissed of bear that got it's leg chopped off in a trap. It'll sit in its cave for a long time starin' at that stump, waitin', plannin', schemin' for that day he can pounce on the hunter that put that trap there and not once consider that the bear himself was the one dumb enough to step in it. That's `cause some critters don't know how dumb they is, and a bear is always gonna be a bear just like some folks is just gonna be who they is no matter how eddy cated, sophisticated, or fancified they become-I reckon there's a little bear in all of us. So it's good to keep that in mind when you go tryin' to mend things.

But it don't matter none, once you get a start, to degauss that magnetic memory field, or neuter that negative charge that's sittin' right ready on top of some brain pan it takes some doin'.

Remember, everybody is in a hurry to do nothing and get there just in time so when it's over you can start up once again.

GET SOME POLISH
Mission #72GSP

Hey folks, I was just goin' through some common issues that could lead to premature damnatory stuff. Doc Wiley'd done some research on a quote that's bugged me since I first heard it. Here's it is:

"If you are irritated by every rub how will you be truly polished?"

So I sent Doc Wiley on a fact findin' mission to set this in a sort of context for my research. Here's what his report said:

REPORT ON POLISH, or The Polish is in the Shine-My expeiences in the men's room at the Grand Fancy Restaurant all expenses courtesy of the Soul Salvation Center.

In an effort to obtain information about the conept of polish I sought out an expert in the field. A shoeshine man. They are relatively rare in ordinary society and therefore sought out, and found one who could provide information on this concept.

Here's what I discovered:

I took a woman out on a date. She was someone I met at the grocery store, and her personality was to a certain degree insufferable. In fact, she would not remain silent for more than thirty seconds. She had opinions on everything from the decor of the restaurant, my attire, and, after telling her my duties at the Soul Salvation Center, and my medical education began baiting me, as if I were a flunky quack. The insults came fast and frequent. I ordinarily would have left her there. However in an attempt to complete this mission endured her banter. Was it Zanenna talk that she was speaking? Note to Seeney: Please evaluate recordings. After the fourth glass of wine I had to to pee. (Note to reader all missions are duly recorded for future reference).

I excused myself and went to the lavatory.

The ancient white haired lavatory attended said. He wore a stylish graphite smock with his name stitched in white cursive lettering, Benny, and a neatly folded rag draped over his left shoulder.

"What?" The man in the Navy Blue blazer, and one too many Manhattan's asked as he walked past him and began to unzip his rumpled trousers.

"Your shoes, sir. Your shoes look like they could use a buff." Benny said softly.

Blue blazer looked at the bathroom attendant then at his footwear. His cowboy boots were a bit scuffed. But big freaking deal, for the prices this joint charged, why add to it with a wise guy in the can trolling for extra coin?

"My shoes are fine," he said and proceeded to relieve myself.

"A little shine adds to a wonderful evening." Benny said.

"No thanks." I said firmly and stood in front of one of the six urinals separated by foot long strips of metal so one pisser couldn't leer at the fellow next him's praphenalia.

"Take care not to soill the spash guard, sir." Benny said.

"Can't you see I'm tryin' to take a piss here?" Damn this guy wouldn't shut up and let me piss if I didn't tip him. "Here, go stand outside and come back in after I've lfet," Blazer gave him a crisp five and went back to getting things going.

"I'm sorry, sir. I cannot leave my station. House rules."

Unable to get his flow going Blazer turned around to face the attendant. He had a spray of freckles across his face like Morgan Freeman and took a step back as the customer approached and pointed his chin to the shoeshine chair. "Perhaps the gentleman could use a respite from the crowd and a bit of time to reflect to get things in order."

There was a Kiwi shoeshine set and a chair against the wall adjacent to the three sinks in front of the huge mirror.

"What're you a friggin' urologist? I gotta go buddy and you're disrupting my concentration. Blazer went into farthest stall and shut it's door, locked it, dropped his jeans and waited. He could see out the crack in the chamber the bathroom's setup.

There was an array of bottles of of lotions, aftershave potions and colognes in front of the mirror. Maybe some sucker would consider putting on a spritz of fragrance, or use one of the combs or hair brushes in the big jar filled with blue fluid. Probably not, because who knew how long those plastic hair care products set there in azure liquid or who used them before and what happened to their hair after they did? No, that was a frightening thought. Lost in reverie, Blazer's flow began. He was thinking about the junk on the counter. The attendant seemed to know that hardly anyone used the hair products and probably hadn't changed the sanitizer in the jar since the restaurant opened its doors all those years ago. I was just tapping off the last few drops when he heard the attendant snap his shoeshine rag like he was buffing the air, implying that if the urinator was so inclined to have his shoes buffed before going back into the swank, overpriced restaurant, he was the man to do it and was intent on getting a tip.

"Are you having a good evening, sir?" Benny said as I righted myself, and studied his face in the mirror.

There was an awkward moment when we both looked at the tip jar and all four eyes lingered longer than either of our comfort zones extended.

The attendant broke the silence. "No sireee, a man don't have no polish he got nothin'." He said

Of course the restroom attendant would expect a tip. But for what? Being a nuisance?

Then again there may be more to this. A reason to spend some extra time in the bathroom, a polite, socially acceptable way to be in a private place away from unpleasant company without going directly to the restaurant's bar in plain sight of one's guest-which would look rude, probably because it was. And Benny seemed to know that.

It had to be less than the price of another two drinks.

How much is it worth to stay in the bathroom if the company you're with is less pleasant, more chatty and mirthless than the old toilet jockey who's got some wise quotes? Who knows, maybe he'd have a few tips on stocks or race track picks, maybe even handicap Superbowl XLV. Maybe polish transcends the banal act of shining someone's shoes, and polish is a gentlemanly form of conduct. Nonetheless, the entire experiece left me with a sense that courtesy and politeness require a skill, patience, and a full bladder.

So I left Sally May Jones sitting at the table staring off into space to listen to what Benny the toilet jockey had to say as he had his boots buffed for the first time in his recollection ever.

I hope this report explains the concept that if you want polish you have to take a lot of rubbing.

VOICES
Reflections on laryngeal lousy loops that play in your head too often...TW

When you hear some people talk their voices make you feel like you're being touched inappropriately. But you say: What the hell? Because being the squiggle on a Jackson Pollock Canvas you are, who knows where you'll be on exhibit next? Then again you may just end up in a museum or the private collection of some jerkoff who likes squiggles. Hey, you could have company, You, Jackson's dollops and, maybe some bent geezer with a bank roll. Not too shabby, but try spending it when your stuck to the wall.

Yes a lot of things run through my mind. Fortunately not the shards of glass of a windshield of car after air bags fail to deploy and the driver's trying to bump you off. And that my friend-and I use the term loosely-is what happened to me today.

I went for a swim, the way I always do, wating for the post man, for a check, or other stuff too. How was I to know, the mail'd be delayed-how could I imagine the condo I live in would be packed with non English speaking construction workers reeking of sour Burrito, Nachos and unwholesomeness? I couldn't. So I swam, dried off, swiped some agua from the water cooler, and made my way to the lobby of this spiffy condominium.

The joint's a few yards from the intracoastal waterway and is home to the true phonies, frauds, sheisteres and crooks, along with a handful of jabronis, mooks, marmalukes a few fanooks and plenty of busybodied a-holes keyhole peeping gazers looking out for some condominium homeowners association violator-which yours truly, is A number one champion of transgressions. In fact I was expecting a notice from the Home Owner's Association about some past due bill I remembered to forget not to pay on time because it was part of my grand schemata to just make a ruckus in light of the overwhelming amount of bureaucratic nonsense a bunch of ulta cockers like to cook up when their not, heralding whores, gasping on respirators, trucking oxygen tanks, early bird diner hopping or sunbathing with their fuzzy beauty of a beast grand offspring. Yecch.

I have to go...there's a knock on the door. I avoided the stench of one place to end up in another...whoops. There it goes again-

In-Laws and Outlaws

The Geniuses: Can they be wrong, ever, about anything?

Everyone who has ever had an in-law, knows what I'm talkng about. They aren't relatives, no-not at all, rather semi-rellies. You MUST be semi-polite to semi-relatives or your spouse will, on some level take it, the subject being it-an attitude, nuance, thready toned: "There's nothing the matter," cold shoulder attitude women use when they're pissed off but don't want to go into details if-and I mean IF you cross that invisible barrier. Invisible barrier? What's that? I am going to tell you that women can project this electrifying field of vibage that isn't quite negative, nasty or mean, rather a vibrating sense of unwholesomeness-as if there was a minor tremor of the earth but she chose to ignore it on account it was irritating, but not irritating enough to cause any real damage and the washing machine won't get thrown off its track, and the vegetable tray in the refrigerator isn't stinky, or you left the toilet seat up.

So you need to tread carefully when you discuss any in-lawage topics because, after all, it's your spouse's family and a lot of people take that stuff seriously.

D.D. CROSS

SOCIAL MEDIA ASSHOLERY
Global Idiocy, the Plague of the 21st Century

So you're bored and decide to go to the Facebook and look at the pictures and all the nifty comments people got. Everyon's gotta tell you what they's doin', where they're at, and blah, blah, blah. You read some of this stuff on the Facebook, and wonder if these computer faces and names that live in cyberspace, I think that's near Des Moines, have any sense whatsoever what they're doin'?

I know, I know, you heard enough of my hell stories, but hang on. When I was in Hades, I found out that the devil keeps tabs on all the folks on earth. Yep, he's got this big ole super duper computer that keeps a record of every keystroke on the computer, every post, every itty bitty thing you do in the corporeal world you can bet you're eternal sould Satan's supercomputer can jiggle up you're whole life. What I don't get is people givin' up all their secrets so easy to some company, Facebook that is, and even puttin' up picutres of themselves too. I look at the book of faces and see folks ramblin' on about one thing or another, one political thing with all the photoshopped pics like they's tryin' to win a Nobel prize. Last time I used that Googly thing there weren't no prizes for Facebook posts. Satan, I discovered gets a kick out of the armchair philosophers who think they got it all figured out. They're his favorites.

Damn geniuses, all of them. It's amazing how the same, brilliant quote, is flashed by so many people about some cutesy aphorism or another within a short span.

The most adorable cliche's with kittens playing the piano about how life should be lived if only you acted or they acted or the world was round and puppies farted a few chords in the key of cuddle. Shut the fuck up morons. All of the cute quotes, expressions, phrases have not only been said, rephrased, requoted as their own, but look so damn stupid they make that picture you primped for look as legit as a Republican presidential nominee when he says: "I believe we should all pay our fair share," Yeah, right.

So I left Facebook and had some coffee, stared at my computer and smacked it. Damn thing has an attitude. Stinkin' computers.

Doc Wiley's into some funk. I don't right know what it is, but savin' souls is hard work. Harder than doctorin' so I reckon he may be close to the burnout. I send him off on missions he don't even know are missions and ask him to write down to keep him busy. Why?

C'mon dummies, you know this: The idle mind is the devil's workshop.

So it's important for me to look after him. After all he could be just step away from eternal damnation. I gotta keep tabs on him real close on account he's come too close to Satan's slick and sneaky ways.

Best way to find out what's in his head's to get him to make notess. I sure's don't want him to land hisself in Hades, but after lookin' at some of the stuff on his Facebook page...Hoowee, Ole Mister Mephistopeles is tappin' one hoof and a waitin'. Collsarn boy's gettin' dumbstruck from all the evil. Go on see for yourself...

D.D. CROSS

TRIP'S TRIP TO THE GROCERY STORE
Amalgamation, Ruminations and Frustrations

Man is this infuriating...What? It's this: I'm fussing around with the coffee machine, feeding it dimes and quarters waiting for my brew to come through. NOTHING. I've already put a buck fifty, now another quarter, and the damn thing's got an attitude. Shit on a stick. Finally I hear the coins click, click, click into place, and it was like a slot machine in Vegas...I'm missin' the place. The strip, the hookers, the action. Shit. Hey look at that the coffee machine's hit three cherries, JACKPOT, I won a cup of coffee...finally. Now another ten minutes for it to deliver. I can wait. What the hell?

I was just about ready to let loose a blast of wind when I hear the dry, fake cough of some woman standing behind me. She's self-consciously staring at the bakery goods, which, she could hardly afford in that dietary sense because any crumb would just be an addition to her saddlebags. We're not talking Roy Roger's steed here, we're talking more Elephant Man upper thigh and hippo buttocks. Yeah, this fortyish dame was checking me out at the supermarket. I know about these things.

Which brings me to a pivotal portion of our mind's activities: what do people exect, why, and does it matter?

Life is a series of unmet expectations, and I ask myself often why bother. Let me think about this, go on, read:

Like a game show contestant with a parting gift her eyes lit up and she pissed herself. Is that the expression, goal, all-time life's grandest moment, or some dubious plunge into the abyss of rancid decay, and expectation of all that can ever be achieved?

So I asked myself: "Why?"

As if some grand cloud swooped down from the heavens-if of course you're inclined to believe in anything-and scooped me up, held me and gave me comfort that all was not for naught. I would have pissed myself too, but the urge was purged and sat there crossed legged in some Far Eastern Meditory pose, as if some grand camera was taking a cosmic photo. And it was then, at that very moment when the celestial shutterbug clicked it's clicker and froze me for time immemorial as another sucker who'd taken the ride of expectation. And then, I knew very well that we were all here for a reason, mine, was perhaps to share with you this most unwholesome revelation, so here goes:

I'll have each of these folks I've met upon the Yellow Brick stream of consciousness, because that is, after all the crosstown traffic of dueliing neruons leave us with after the daily chores, hassles, worries, frets, frats frittatas, fandangos fears and futile fidgeting leaves us with. The that being this and here are the words of mentally meanderings of most provocative minions of mindfulness who've woven wondrous weird wired wobegon adventures.

Eustice, who'd-I don't know how many times I've said it-died a few years back. By some miracle of error, of the sort only humans could screw up managed to survive with a belief that life had some purpose. Did he discover something obscured from our ordinary belief that we are here to do a deed or seek some answer be it divine, mundane, rote, rotisserie kabob on some survivalist grill solely to procreate like aunt's bees, and all the animal kingdom or did we, as humans, have some redeeming reason to revile in life's most ridiculous questions for which no answer could be questions? Conundrums abound when things settle down and time left alone away from phone or some other task chore or endeavor-To wonder, perhaps, a waste that's not chaste rather curious imbroglios leading alas to a place where our minds weren't meant to wander?

So I posed this question in a way such as this: What the hell are we here for and no it's no quizz-that was in case my friend was a wiz. But again another question arose, and all of my brain cells gummed up and they froze. What's a friend? That depends on your state? A relationship with a person you've met, a stranger whose concepts and notions blend well, or someone whose tales of horror and woe meet you half way as you compare or you fight-Need a journey between people be based on a fight or do people lock eyes and have love at first sight. The levels of friends to outsiders seem strange the sexual strains some leave you with stains, but ideas and gifts are laden with thrifts some wholly based on material rifts.

Lost as I am, I devised some grand plan and sought out the answers to some of my dancers that tickled my cerebral zone some like antlers, turned outside in, right under my skin of my scalp, oh they itched and rubbed and they itched and scratching my mind was a son of a bitch. It came to me then as it often does friend, you've followed me so far, therefore I assume you're a curious seeker which you can hardly defend. Just what lie behind door number two is it some grand prize or hint or a clue? Surprise yourself, please with the Karmic disease of ideas and thoughts let free at all costs but the time you invest in taking this test.

Why are you here? Why am I?

Am I making it clear that words have reasons and rhymes for all seasons and each one occurs every day. I ask you one thing, well wait maybe two-If the answer you find is remotely near true, would you share it with someone or keep to yourself, or maybe develop a fictional fast talking elf?

Listen up buddy let me be clear, this riveting ride through my mind isn't clear. My fingers are typing, my thoughts are on hold. I'm writing this down as if I'm doin' as I'm told. All control of ideas abated indeed, maybe I'd smoked some incredible weed? No that's not the case if that's what you believe-but dismissive of questions quirks curious heeds, the ready made answers that fit with a squeeze-Into packets of concepts to make you at ease, with what you've accepted as the way things just are-Because life is simple and you go with the flow, and follow the rules, and all will be well, and there is no question of heaven or hell.

What is existence, but an abstract subsistence. An absence of duties or tasks none at all the idle mind sits when asked it dispenses what's gathered and sorted by all of your senses. But lie to you sometimes eyes, nose ears

and throat, what you see and believe may be a fine hoax-
But what am I saying? Just a rambling rant, but hang on
now stranger take deep breath like a dog and set back to
just pant. Are your listening?

Trip Wiley, note to self.

I Awoke into Scary Land
Trip's trippy day

He laid there staring at the ceiling, or so he thought. It was actually the back of his eyelids that his mind's eye saw. There were patterns of light that danced around as he tried opening his lids which felt like wet curtains at an X-rated movie theatre. Crusty, that's how they felt, as if the lashes had been coated with some foul, rancid, gum that held his eyes shut. He focused all of his being into opening his eyes shutting down all movement from his toes on up, and breathed shallow, albeit oxygenating breaths.

There was no telling how long he was vectoring his entire self-whatever that was-on this very simple, and most ordinary task. Was it a dream? Had he still been asleep, and if so was it a nightmare which carried over into wakefulness? The harder he tried opening his eyes the brighter the kaleidoscope of colors became and a sense of panic grew from somewhere deep in his mind. But it didn't feel like his mind, something was awry-he couldn't put his finger on it, but he couldn't feel his fingers, toes, or for that, anything. Something was horribly wrong, and the more he thought of what it could be the brighter and more intense the colors and patterns became. A show of angry fireworks danced across the back of his eyelids like riveting bursts of lightning among dense clouds during a festival where he was the sole viewer. Finally he gave up and became still, so still his breathing was all he was aware of and then the rancid stench of decay coated the hairs within his nose, and made their way to that part of his brain-the mind that wasn't his-and whoever's skull he was in. It couldn't be real no, not real a dream and to awake would wash away this state of non being and then, he tasted something, What?

His tongue had filled his mouth which, like his eyes he could not open. He wanted to scream but the place in the mind where the impulse to act was lost. Shit, at least he could curse to himsself and he thought it hard. Harder hardest louder ruder meaner finally there was a jolt and every cell of his body exploded into millions of brigher lights than the Fourth of July displaying behind his eyelids. It was pain, not just pain but some thoroughly encompassing menace of destruction which would surely be a sign that something was being destroyed, gnawed by vermin, burned, his skin peeled off slowly and acid dripped on the bare layers of exposed nerve. Wake up, wake up. He said to himself but it wasn't his voice at all rather that of someone outside of the shell he'd been in for hours, but it couldn't have been more than a minute and any sense of time or it's passage was lost to the sights, sounds and senses by what came next. Absolute and complete darkness. Everything stopped. Blackness, cessation of the smell, freedom from pain, nothing. He couldn't find the mind that had moments earlier was jailer and jail itself. Was he dead? Was this an afterlife, a freedom from all corporeal existence? The elimination of all things sensory? No, he was thinking, he had a mindfulness that surely if he were dead would be gone along with all the horrible things which came before. What was this netherplace? And then a rustling sound followed by murmurs, was it his heart, had it been beating all along and he was just hearing it, sensing it? No there were voices...

"Dude, wake up, man," a voice said.

It was a dream, wasn't it?

BEGGING THE QUESTION
How is the reality revealed in our dreams less real than a trip to the grocery store?

Do our dreams fade away for a reason, or are the remnants of what occurred in our mind's eye invisible for as a physiologic function? What would that funtion be, adn why? For what reason would that part of our mind revealed in dream be obscured from wakeuful thinking and examination? The ideas, thoughts, ideations exist in some state, why not in another where they can be examined, studied, dissected?

Imagine having access to the places you visit while asleep. Can the occasional nightmare be too horrible to endure in a conscious state? Maybe be joyous revelations too exhilerating to tap into during the day. Questions, questions, questions.

Do we have some incontrovertible evidence suggesting that what our thoughts which are unthinkable in the waking state may be some indication as to a reality which exists, so profound, so bizarre, scathing, treacherous that it's withheld from our wakeful journeys? Does some mammalian structure predating civilization exist dating back to a time when we fought or fled the monstrous realities of every day life? As we painted on walls of caves, before fires were discovered and animal hide kept us warm our intransigence remained in check by our own physiology. The fight or flight mechanism governed by our adrenal pituitary axis, whereby our eyes or ears would sense an awfulness and quickly-rather immediately invoke a cascade of events leading to a secretion of catecholamines, the neurotransmitters riveting through our circuitry to charge us up to run or do battle? Diverting oxygenated blood to areas where muscles needed to flail, to our hearts to pump fiercely, to heighten an awareness of our senses so we'd know when, where and how best to deal with life's terrors as if they were routine.

WE'RE NOT SO FAR FROM THE CAVE
What's 20,000 years give or take a century or two when you can't get a cell phone signal?

The primal urgency of cave dwellers has been lulled into dormancy by the niceties of civilization. We're all hard wired the same-that brutal fight or flight essence of humanity-it has not dissolved. Nope, not yet, not in our lifetimes. We try to conceal, remove. or dress up that part of ourselves from the base, crude, and sometimes frightening impulses, but they have a way of showing up, sometimes in unwelcome ways. Think road rage here.

We can manage them-to a degree-for the most part-but we're never more than a few heartbeats away from the savage beneath the suit. The house training of a few thousand years hasn't changed us in ways which may not at all be consistent with who or what we are. Animals. Base, tawdry, hungry, horny, sweating, fighting, fucking beasts whose distance from those caves is a flinch from the sight of a mastodon, yet strapped down by conditioning, and domestication of social mores. Repressed, and by the charters, rules, regulations, laws, and niceties of a so-called civilized world. Put to rest those uniquely human qualities we're physiologically designed with, but instead, by some grand design subdued. Is it a convenience that our appetites are so difficult to control, our curiosities remain intact to keep us aware and wondering what lurks behind a tree, or has society sucked the life out of our very nature, kept us-with the mores of morons-prisoners of our own flesh to merely bow down to the domesticizations that make the dysfunctional admixture of cultures and our selves no grander than they had been when we dwelt in caves. Fuck them all we are animals and I want my Purina.

HE REALLY DID CUT OFF HIS JOHNSON!
Another schmuckless schmuck?

Doc Wiley tole me this dumb ole story, but it had somethin' to do with that mission a spell back, here's what he said:

"This guy carrying a knapsack walks into a doctor's office and says: "I was born a woman in a man's body, cut off my penis, balls, and make me a vagina."

So go on, what happened? Trip keep goin'

"The doctor leans back in his chair, takes a deep breath, and says: "Asshole, you'd make one ugly fucking bitch. But if you really want to be a woman, you'll have to follow the proper protocol. I'll schedule a psychiatric evaluation, and we'll take it from there. Have you talked this over with your parents?"

I ask him what happened and Trip goes'n tells me what the kid said:

"My mother says that it's a great idea," the young fellow said to the doctor.

I get me to wonderin' if this was part of our mission, and nodded my head for Doc Wiley to keep goin'

"Oh, and I suppose that your father has an opinion too?"

So how'd it go Trip, what happened?

"The young fellow shrugged his shoulders and shook his head from side to side before exploding into a litany of what an asshole his father was, and that all men, were scum. He says that having his dick cut off, and becoming a woman has nothing to do with his father, rather the FACT that his mother, a victim of a horrible divorce because his father cheated on her and punished him for being a fuck up was irrelevant."

I say to Trip: "Who's the mother?"

"The young man reached into his knapsack and took out a dead cat and placed it on the doctor's desk and stepped back.

This is when I knew it wasn't some dumb joke, or fable, it was a real story, and Doc Wiley knew the doctor on account I think it migh've been him because this is what he said:

"The doctor looks down at it and says: "What's this?"

Trip said that the kid tole the doc: "It's my mother's calling card. She said you'd understand."

And there it was, this was that lady speakin' Zanenna talk. I knew because this is what the doc finally said:

"Oh, it's Tuffy" he said nodding his head. "We can schedule your surgery for noon tomorrow."

Doc Wiley smiled over at me, and said that there lady was plum looney tunes and we ought be careful on account we could get our johnson's chopped off by a troup of Zannena yappin' man haters.

Hoowee, I reckon that I misread a client, and these Zannennas from Scorneo were really out there, in bigger numbers than I thought, and they were not only goin' to hell, they were gonna take a heap of johnson's with `em.

This here's when I reckon that I was gonna cross paths with the likes of one of them folks again, and I ought not let too many intervening circumstances get in my thinker brain's gears and gum up my thoughts.

In the mean time I knew there was cases to work on and missions to do. In fact this was so imprtant I had to dig through the files, and go through all my recollections.

Eustice Does SERIOUS Research
The Grand Scam

I got me to doin' good deeds on account that's what I'm supposed to do or I will go right on back to hell. You know the deal, if you're bad, you go to hell? Well I died and instead of seein' the bright white light saw this big ole dark blur and went tumblin' through a tunnel. Oh I saw myself leave my body. It was on the operatin' table-the anesthesia must've gone bad-on account they called it a code. I think them folks down there, I was lookin', down from the ceiling was talkin' in code, were tryin' to bring me back. Didn't work, and I was in Hades. Yep. There's a few books about it, on account I figured out how to get out. But the deal was, if I did leave hell I had to perform good deeds. Then again that's what the lawyer said after I sued the hospital for fuckin' me up and landin' me in a coma for a spell. Good money too!

REMEMBERIN' MY FIRST MISSION
How Things Come Back and Bite You in the Ass..

So there's this divorced lady in some yuppy neighborhood that wants to get even with her ex. He's a fella that married a younger, prettier gal and was supposed to be havin' a good old time. I was supposed to show this codswallopin' fella the wickedness of his ways and this is the way it went:

Mah lawyer man says that he had a special job for me that'd help me dispell the ghoulish, decay I was supposed to feel for all the money I got. It didn't, so

I got these missions. I figure it best I go see the aggrieved ex and calm her down on account I used to do my share of ass banditry' and'd get mah self in some real trouble. This was, probably the same deal, the fella abandons the wife and kids for some younger gal and has a good ole time, heck. I did it twice and John Q tracked me down both times for skippin' out on the alimony. Maybe this was all I had to do, track the subitch down and have a good talkin' to with him. Yep, that simple.

Hoowee was I wrong. I met this woman at her house. The one her stray husband must've bought. It was a biggen. Sprawled out with a big ole circular drive. A fancy Land Rover parked up front and ivy growin' up side the walls of the place. There was a colored fella ridin' one of them sit down lawn mowers and a pool service truck there too. I rang the doorbell on one of the big ole oak doors and after a spell this short, frumpy woman, I thought it was the help at first, but could see over he head that it wasn't-there was some foreign lookin' lady in a maid's costume vacuum sweepin' the floor. I guess answerin' doops wasn't her job. This gal was all super theatrical and starts talkin, usin' her hands and body like she was in a play. She said:

"I'm so glad you came. My lawyer said you were the right man for the job that you could find truly evil men and show them the light. And let me tell you," she kept talkin' as she led me into the house. I felt like I was in a basketball court on account the place was so big it echoed and this woman's voice was deep and spooky like she was talkin' from the bottom of an oil drum.

"Sure ma'am. I'm in the business of trackin' down evil doers and settin't them on the right path." I said.

"I don't think my ex will ever be on the right path. He's bipolar, he's a drunk and has left me for another woman. Look at me, look at me, am I not all the woman a man could want?" She didn't stop a beat and echoed on, "I want that bastard living under a bridge and every penny he's ever stolen, that drunkard." She kept goin' Jeez, does this ever end. We was in the kitchen and she set me up a place at the table and offered me a drink explainin' that there was plenty of liquor her husband left behind.

"No sense lettin' it go stale," I said thinkin' she might just fall for that.

She nodded. "Yes, of course let me get you something, gin all right?"

"Whatever you got'll do," I said. Hell yeah gin'd be just dandy, besides, like I said, I gotta keep the spirit goin'.

I looked at the gal who'd put a glass on the table, poured a finger of gin and set the bottle on the counter. She was in her middle ages and I could tell that she hated, and I don't mean just hated, but spoke about men the way folks that lived under Hitler spoke about that dead Nazi. Well to this gal, her ex husband was WORSER than Hitler. I looked the gal over, sure enough she was leavable, in fact I would've walked out her right then iffen she didn't offer me up a drink or three. By the fourth gin she looked better than the wicked witch of the whatever and I listend to her tale or sorrow. Must notta been too bad on account the house she was livin' in was bigger than two of my trailer parks and you could probably land a Cessna in her kitchen. She had long dyed black hair, I could tell 'cause the roots were white and a narrow forehead like that chimp scientist from the movie: Planet of the Apes. She had pasty skin that must've felt like Elmer's Glue and lips as thin as tiny pencils-the kind I used to swipe from golf score sets over to the Country Club, which, this short, stubby bad hair dye job woman belonged too-I saw the sticker on the Land Rover. She wore jeans and a red shirt to show off her breastesses-why else wear a shirt that tight? Unless of course it done shrunk...but she had a maid who was cleanin' up the place, so that must notta been the case. There was a cellular phone in a sack clipped to her belt and the belt's buckle was a big metal ex, designed just like the ring she wore on her marriage band finger, it could've been a wedding ring but I examined it real close and it was a bunch of X's all he way around. She must've seen me starin' on account she said: "This is to signify that I am woman. I do not need a man in my life and that drunken bastard has taken money and hidden it offshore. I want you to find it. I am sure he has it hidden and know that you will find it. It's for the children." She harumphed. Yep, people actually close a speech with one of those. It's as if a pillow got tossed and all the foam went out of it then sprung back real quick. Harumph.

"Yes, ma'am," I said, holdin' out my liquor cup.

Just then the doorbell goes off. I swallow my gin and while the gal, goes to answer runs to see who's there I take a long pull off the Bombay Saphire. Hmm, what's a man with good taste in gin doin' a stumpy little dwarfy monkey faced gal doin' with fine booze? I was wipin' my lips off and layin' the bottle down real careful not to make no noise and glance over at bad dye job. Hoowee, I almost retched it on up. I ain't never seen a tookas as big as that one. It, her caboose, was like the whole moon itself, an if the moon was made of cheese this one, by the way it jiggled was made outta Mozzerella or Ricotta cheese. I settle back in my chair and watched her walk back with another gal. Was I lookin' at that Rachel Madow plus? Or some marine drill sargent with a pair of hooters? I hear `em chucklin' and could tell bad dye was fake laughin' it was that grating, mirthless, artificial sound that people make when they act like somethin's funny when it ain't.

Hoowee, this was gonna be a hoot. Find some dude and then find out where he socked his loot a way? I didn't really think so. But this gal was a tough one to disagree with and I liked the free gin. Besides, I was thinkin' to mah self I ain't never seen a real live troll before and this was it.

I go on over and check out the new wife. I got me to thinkin' that if mah mission was to save souls it probably wasn't a good place to start on acount that lady didn't seem to have no soul.

Old Poop...Again
*Bad Pennies Never Go Away (They don't
copper out either)...*

I had to take my neighbor over to the doctor a couple weeks ago and he did some stuff to her. She's all better but sweared she'd never go back to him on account he grabbed her ass. She also didn't like the goods at the dollar store next poor at the shoppin' plaza. Hey, you can't please everyone anyway-besides, that was probably the first fella that grabbed her tush in years.

You remember me tellin' you about old Poop. He's that drunkard doc on his way to Hades. Don't tell nobody on account that'd be speakin' ill of the damned or somethin on account that'd wreck his credibility in purgatory. So far, the fella's credibility has been in. It's in credibly bad. Old Poop had some troubles with the revenoors and sort of forgot to pay taxes and they came and was gonna tow his Mercedes Benz last week. I was right there in the office when a couple revenoors came in and said they wanted their money. Poop said: "I don't owe you nothin' look around this isn't my offish." he said just like that.

Old Poop had been visitin' with the Captain earlier. As in Captain Morgan we'd had a few tipples. Pooper had a few more than me on account he's a professional. Me, I'm just a patient and have the patience to deal with

Poop's tall tales and stories of wonder. They're stories of wonder on account I get to wonderin' if any of `em are true. Either way, he always has plenty of rum in his office and all sorts of other nifty things. One of those things was that fancy car he'd let me wash and drive when he and the Captain spent too much time together, which was a pretty lot. You see old Poop has a special relation with the Cap-that's just fine with me, and I like drivin' the fancy car and listenin' to some good banjo music on the car's fine stereo. I wonder if the revenoors are gonna take the CDs and all when they tow the car away. It got me to thinkin' so I went out and looked at the tow truck, thinkin' maybe I could sneak into the car and swipe the albums and be done. That'd been real simple but when I got over to the parking space behind the office Poop was out there yackin' with the revenoors. Let me tell you this: They, the gummit men were lookin' a might peeved. Poop, had gun!

Holy shit. I was ready to turn tail and head out, but thought since these guys was out here I'd duck back into the office for a jolt or two of rum. Big mistake. I'd taken my first slug of liquor when the back door bursts open and Poop comes tumblin' in like a hobo gettin' tossed off a box car. He was pissed off and then some. The revenoors was real mad too.

"Do you have a permit for that gun?" One of the revenoors had Poop's pistol and was starin' at it.

Poop was sittin' on the floor and had handcuffs on behind his back.

The other revenoor, a colored fella was standin' there watchin' his partner and lookin' at old Poop. He was just shakin' his head from side to side and pulled his lower lip out of his face with his fingers and let it snap back. Poop saw this and said real loud: "What're you doin' Negro?"

That colored fella turned two shades of white and hauled off and planted his wing tip right on Poop's chin sendin' him over backwards. I reckon the handcuffs dug into his back `cause Poop shouted: "I'm gonna sue you're rousy brack ash. Do you know who I am, do you?"

I guess the other revenoor, the one with Poop's gun got a bit startled and figured manhandlin' somebody wasn't too smart on account there was a witness and that witness was yours truly. He looked me in the eye in that, you best shut up way most cops do and helped Poop get up. He made some kinda motion to the colored guy to help him when all of a sudden the whole collsarn room went kablooey!

Old Poop let out a gush of gut wind that was maybe a 9 on the rectal Richter scale. Hoowee did that razzle last...it went on and on knockin' pens off the desk, discombobulatin' the picures on the wall, and I'll tell you, I think the building's foundation must've shaken.

The two revenoors went into chokin' and gaggin' and one of `em the uncolored guy actually started pukin' runnin' for the door.

Hoowee, I just grabbed the bottle of Captain Morgan's and ran. When I got to the highway to take a look see what happened the collsarn shoppin' plaza'd gone into crumblin' like there WAS an earthquake.

I went back to the trailer park and finished the rum off and went to sleep. That night I put on the TV news, and sure enough old Poop's place was leveled by a freak earthquake leavin' two men seriously injured and one foot doctor behind bars.

But I know what really happened on account an hour later I found out what bars they was talkin' about, and old Poop was right there sippin' his drink. It was his favorite bar. The Mercedes was parked outside.

It just goes to show that some folks have lotsa power they don't use.

Qualifiers and Quality People
Are you friends or friend(ish)?

I got me a mission out of the blue one day. A gal came to see me, and told me a story. It went like this:

In a condo parking lot somewhere in South Florida a snowbird widower with his new lady friend are parked in front of the condominium's front door. The old dude is an 80ish good old boy from Midwestiana, and the sort who tosses his weight around as if he had the pounds sterling in the bank to match what he's got on the scale. He's a chubby blowhard, but that's his business.

Ordinarily folks'd nod their head and say hi when when they'd cross paths with the guy. Chit chat a little about politics and stocks and sports-superficial shit. His braggadocio isn't just boorish, it's beyond bilious. So, big whoop, another geezer in the Sunshine State Stupidland, hi, howaryou-that's it. No real stop-and-chats, nope, not worth the time to hear this cat ramble on about how great of a guy he is. Fuck him.

So she's comin' back to her plave from the store, she's driving a big ole fancy Jaguar, all content and singin' along to herself to the music. Get it, no big deal, see mister white bread milk toast in the parking lot. Big deal. So she gets out of the car. Mizz Jewess sees the guy and while she's gathering the groceries from the back seat, the dude swings his Town Car around and rolls down the window. She says: "Hey there how ya doin'," in a whoop ti do tone.

"Howdy," he says.

The gal., bags in her hands, goes over to the Town Car as if she's glad to see the widowed, what she believed was a nice guy, and gives him a peck on the cheek. The white hair's got an old lady in the passenger seat. Probably going to take his willy out for a Cialis strut

I think to myself, not knowin' if the guy's a relatively low level perv. A boner pill poppin' jolly joy rider out to get laid enjoyin' the South Florida Sun, hittin' on a right fine lookin' gal. Nope. There was more goin' on here.

This here's common: A regular hick when he wants to be, or a political bully expert who ran big businesses at others expense. Yep, a regular genuine, artificial snowbird blowhard up to no collsarn good.

So the woman turns her back, saying in a nice, sing-song, Dolly Sunshine tone: "Nice to see you're back," tone and walks back to her Jag-she must've forgotten something the way she tole me the tale.

Then, the geezer's lookin' at her ass-she sees him in the reflection someplace. I woulda done so too. But that's not proper.

The geeze says without preamble: "Ahm goin' over to the other coast to see my other Jewish friend," matter of factly.

"Really?" Mrs. me says. She says it in that tone of what the fuck did you just say.

He looks over at her and has that look someone on a tightrope does when they notice the twine's starting to come undone and there ain't no safety net.

"Did you really just say that?" She says.

I'd have to wager that the broad the old dude was with was Jewish too. She was just his condo pussy so, he initially forgot to introduce her -I figured he just had her with him so he could prove his aging manhood-and didn't give a shit what she had to say.

But there it was, that same old same old anti-semite shit. You get a lot of that, and it's low level noise so it doesn't even register on your Jewdar. But it's there pal, trust me on that. Personally I'd have gotten in his face with a glib: "Hey how's my GENTILE friend?" But didn't because morons will be morons forever and this guy's forever could be an hour, maybe less-But...

Mrs. Hebrew was miffed. I mean really taken aback by this seemingly harmless comment.

When people call you their friend, you figure your their friend without any qualifier, like this is my: Retarded friend, or my black friend. or my oriental friend.

So I gather from these qualifiers in friendships things as a way people have of categorizing people to fit into their stereotypes. My reckoning is that this guy hates-that's sort of strong-rather, doesn't care for Negroes, I've heard him call black people niggers, so that pretty much is the deal. I wasn't REALLY convinced, at least till yesterday that Jews were among that group he isolated-in his mind-like most do, folks unlike himself. I figure he's got some image as money grubbing, bagel eating, yarmulke wearing, whining figure that sites in his puny brain and has been there for all his life.

Yep. Qualifiers are a sure fire way to know things. In particular when someon uses a qualifier to describe someone that you think you know isn't someone you'd really care to know. Other than a cursory, nod. Maybe a: "Hi," and then to yourself say: You fucking bigoted asshole.

Nope, people who qualify people are not quality people. Fuck `em.

The old dude in his Town Car and gal in the parkin' lot?

She said: "Really?" Had a shocky look, almost frozen in place, hrt face drained of color, and noticably she freaked out, in that, I can't believe what I just heard sort of way.

Next time someon pulls one of those cracks, she ain't gonna freak out. Nope. Now she'll know what to do. Thanks to a visit to the Soul Salvation Center.

ROBOTS
Are we that stupid to have given the machines so much power?

Hooweee. Used to be a time when you could call somebody at a company about your bill and talk to a person. That was a time that long since passed. Nowadays you call up someone like the electric company or even worse, the phone company, and you get this whole riga maroll tellin' you to press number one for your balance and number two for somethin' else and on and on until you go collsarn nuts.

I was tryin' to get on line with mah com puter on account it tweren't workin' right, and I reckoned it was the connection. This is what hapened:

I called on up the phone company, sure enough the first question the robot voice asks if I wanna speak to them in English or Spanish to press number this or that. Dang! This is `Merica, the collsarn computers don't even wanna talk to you in English, so I press #1. Now, I get a whole long list of choices and none of them got a button sayin' `If you wanna talk to an operator,' so I just wait and wait. Next thing I know (between you and me I was watchin' TV so they weren't wastin' my vaulable time), next thing I know I get the "If you would like to make a call, beep beep beep beep beep," sound of you have been disconnected and "if you would like to try again" bull pucky.

So, I have another brewsky and let er rip..same riga maroll, and I just go into pushin' buttons. Finally some lady gets on the phone with a accent that's so hard to understand I say: "Where you at? Pittsburgh? She just chuckles and says: "We are not to be allowed to be telling you the loctaion that we are at."

Okey dokey I say to myself. Mebbe you can help me figger out how to get my computer workin'. This potatoes in her mouth woman goes to mumble somethin' about goin' to the web site. I say I cay ain't got to the web site on account mah com puter connection ain"t workin'. I figure it's that simple, right? I'll get transferred to technical support. Sure enough old Miss Mumbly puts me on hold and next thing I know I'm disconnected again. So I call back and get another person-mind you this, I'm up to six beers, and two reruns of Matlock have come and gone. I finally talk to some dude in a country I ain't never heard of. Remberin' these people don't have last names, I follow his instructions and vo walla, my computer is workin' fine. By then, I forgot what I wanted to use the com puter for and realize why `Merica is so pissed off. All these jobs are pawned off to either machines or some dummies in other countries.

There ought to be a law about these robots and answering the phone. They're rude. I mean really rude-I been dissed by lots a humans but now there are uppity computers. Try this on: If you are having trouble please try your call again later. That was the last straw-I took the phone bill, ripped it up and pee'd on it. Fuck `em. Hey robots, go fuck yourself.

Ten minutes ago there was a knock on the door. I ignored it, the way I ignore most knocks on my door. But it didn't stop. I go look out through the peep hole and there's this big ole machine standin' out on my porch. Shee yattt, I go get my shotgun and put a shell in the chamber. I figure I'll intimidate the robot.

Let me tell you this, robo didn't care. So I shot it, I shot the robot. It didn't do anything. It came into my trailer and started cattywompin' me one two three like I was a crumb and next thing I know I got robo crap all over me. My ankles and wrists are all hog tied and I hear this robo soundin' voice goin': If you would like customer service press one, if you would like to enquire about your balance press two and on and on and on...it lasted for hours, I missed my favorite TV shows but finally when it was over the smell of burnt air hung there and the robot was gone. I was rubbin' my wrists from where the phone company robot had me subdued and went over to call the cops, the line was dead. Shee yatt, you really can't fuck with these machines, I grabbed my scatter gun again and decided I'd go after that varmint. Yep, that was my plan. But somethin' happened, I stepped in a big pile of robopoop. Yes. I mean really yes the robot left a pile on my floor. It was so thick that my foot got stuck and that's where I am now, stuck knee deep in robot poop.

FLORIDA

Shockingly mundane and absurd
Or, how several decaying electrons can occupy the
same orbital...

Some say that if you look at a map of the US, Florida sticks out like a craggily penis poking into the Caribbean. The fact on the ground in the Sunshine State is that it's not just some bent finger, it's actually a very decrepit, depraved desperate, disenfranchised, doleful, dummy laden, dangling digit.

If the finger's phony polished nail is The Keys and Miami, the area extending up to the distal phalanx up from Dade, through Broward and on through Palm Beach Counties is the tip of the shit stained finger and the grime beneath the nail represents the con artists, crooks, chiropractors, dopers, druggies, douchebags, dingalings, dumbells, wheeler dealer, tinsel toned bronzed broncos riding the wild steer of the road rage ravaged highways of the tropical tundra also known as the wonderful world of whiplash. Law? There are some, but Floridians accept them as mere suggestions and the politicians are the best money can buy.

Best? Florida is the only state where you can spend a year or so in prison for murder but get life for having a bag of grass if you get the wrong cop on the right day who just so happens to plant some corn behind your seat. Florida's weather-year round sunshine-attracts street urchins from around the globe who bask beneath bridges, beg at highway exit ramps and drive home in their Bentley. And that home is more often than not mortaged to the tune of a few mil and has been foreclosed on five years ago. How can a bum with no credit history, no job, a credit score under ten and a history of stiffing everyone but his wife live there? Hell, it's Florida, it ain't the real world and the courts are so backed up with petty lawsuits, you can be sued, adjudicated and put on someone's collection radar for nearly a decade before anything happens. Is Florida the crime state? No. It's the: "I don't give a shit state." And if you really want a cleaner answer it's the `We'll get around to it,' state. So if you need a place to lay low where nobody's going to enforce a judgement against you look no furthere than the likes of OJ SImpson, F. Lee Bailey, Bernie Madoff and watch a few episodes of American Greed. If you really want a big picture of Florida check out that 2000 election...Having a brother who's the Governor helps. And those dangling chads can be tricky.

If you live in Florida, especially South Florida which could be a nation onto itself because no one is really FROM South Florida rather people, all sorts of people go there and just nestle in. Spanish, Haitian, Creole, and a few pockets of non heavily East Coast as in Snooki or the Sitch accented people meander about vengefully because in South Florida, unlike most other places EVERYONE has the right of way-so be careful on the roads.

The roads in South Florida are paved with the essence of the Chiropractic Mafia. Not necessarily the Mafia Mafia, more a loosely knit group of Chiropractors, bottom feeding lawyers, scum bags and fakers who all come together to hike up insurance rates on account of the their multi-level scams including but not limited to bogus bang ups, fender benderitists, runners and dirty cops.

It Don't Matter What Kind of Clock You Got: *Time Treats Us All the Same...*

There's this fella I know who's some kinda doctor. I think he was mentioned earler. I been tryin' to help get him get an ounce of redemtion, but it's been rough. I think he's a specialist or somethin' but ain't quite what it he specializes in except for bein' liqoured up all the time. I got a call from someone that said he needed a look see, and that he was gettin' all goofy on account he talks real strange, and been some sort of mean too.. I checkend in, and sure in enough, it's a fact he is real strange.

This fella I call him Poop, on account he's always makin' doody. Lot's of it, and all day long. In fact he's got some kinda stomach area disease or somethin'. Maybe it's from all the liquor. He had some operation a few years back and says he's all better...sorta. He always argues and gets to yellin', and if you disagree he says: "I gotta take a shit." That leaves me wonderin' if that surgery he had on his guts did but for nothin' because he got to drinkin' more and more. Maybe he got hisself a booze pouch.

He ain't got a lot of folks that like bein' around him 'cause he's always blatherin' and actin' like some high falutin fancy schmancy rich fella. He ain't got but for nothin' on account the revenoors been on his tush for's long as I knowed him. He wears fancy time clocks on his wrist and I swear he got a bunch of `em. They look real expensive and he says they's the real McCoy. B'tween me and you, I think they's knockoffs, but that's juss me, and I wouldn't know `bout that sorta stuff `cause the fanciest clock I got is from that high class place over at the Sears I think it's a Cashio and got these computer numbers on it.

I talked about time earlier, and how you mesure it. It don't matter what kind of clock you use, time treats us all the same.

I like my watch just fine in basic black. Plastic that is. Oh yeah, back to Poop.

He's mad at me this week.

I reckon he's cantankerous cause it's the Holidays, and he's extra drunk and can't get anothr DUI or he goes right to the slammer.

Like I said, I met this guy a spell back before I got dead the first time. He was real fat asshole then, now he's a skinny asshole, and got a hunched back too. Looks like a scrawny vampire with bad teeth. I reckon he's all crumpled forward on account he tends to people's body parts all day and sits on this little stool with folks stinky thingss in his face. Eww. He's got this office in a bad neighborhood where there's plenty of whores and junkies and gang kids roamin' around and, Poop caries a gun. Two guns-one under his shirt, the other on his desk. I go over and visit him from time to time on account he keeps a bottle of Captain Morgan back in his private office next to his Walther PPK. Poop told me he likes that gun a lot on account James Bond's got one just like it. I guess

Poop's a regular double O doc, yep. A regular doctor spy all shakin' and stirred.

I go on over to Poop's doctorin' shop and his secker tarry says: "You haven't paid your co-pay"

"Hell no, I ain't no customer. I'm here to help save the man's soul." I say to the gal, and she just tells me to sit my behind down in the wait room. There's a bunch of old stinky folks in there, and they all got one thing in common. Or maybe two. One is that they prob'ly got some achy part, and the other is maybe that want somethin' to make `em feel better. So that day there's this big ole colored gal sittin't there talkin' on her smart phone. I don't right know why they call `em smart on account they don't do much but I see folks pushin' buttons and yakkin' and all. I get to watchin' this big ole gal when I hear the Pooper.

"Hello," He shouts on out from the hallway and then pokes his head in the wait room, looks at me and nods then over at the gal and says: "How's my Negress today?"

I got to tell you, iffen I was that lady, I'd a right smacked him but good. But she don't say nothin' on account her aches must be real sore. She just blushes in that way darkies do when they get embarrassed. You know like when the clouds go over the moon at night. You know, when your outside tinkerin' with someone's car, as in like stealin' some hub caps on a full moon, and you gotta think somethin' like where the police might be? Well all of a sudden it gets darker, and that's what the big gal did. She went from dark to darker on account maybe Poop made her feel crummy. But that ain't none of my business. I just wanted me some good old Captain Morgan.

"Hey Poop," I say. "Is the skipper in?" That there is code for if the Captain is in.

Poop just looks over at me, shakes his head a bit, waves the darkie in and says, "I gotta take a shit."

The gal behind the counter rolls her eyes up into her head so hard I get to thinkin' maybe her skull cap will burst open from her eyeballs. She finally started breathin' again and told me to take a seat again. I was thinkin' about doin' that on account I could use a new chair over at my trailer. The place, Poop's nastiness, and the booze was lookin' less enticin'. I tried to calm myself.

I picked up a fishin' and boatin' magazine to look at while I waited. It had all these pictures of boats. Poop used to have a boat and I went on it with him once. He got so plastered that it kept running up on the sand bars. I think Poop thought he could order drinks there on account he done drunk all his wine. They wasn't servin' much over there but jammed up motors.

Few months later the revinoors come and took old Poop's boat away. I reckon that was OK because it didn't have no terlet on it and Poop had to make his doody in a bucket. If anyone asked I'd tell `em the boat was a real stinker. I see this fine lookin' model showin' off boat motors and tear out the page. That must've made the secker tarry real made on account she tole me to put the book down.

Just then I hear this lady scream. Holy smokes she wailed like someone done took off a toenail or somethin' without no anesthesia and was havin' a baby-a big one at that-too! Collsarnit, I jumped off my seat and despite that secker tarry bein' all uppity ran back to the examinator rooms and saw that sure enough ole Poop was yankin' off some old gals toenail and she was sittin' in this funny space ship-like chair with her hands clutchin' the sides like she was ridin' a buckin' bronco.

"Poop!" I hollered. "What're you doin' to that gal?" I went over the the heifer and held her arm. She grimaced so hard I thought the corners of her mouth was gonna come off her face.

"Go on buback to where you was," he said. Collsarnit, he said it in the drunkiest of drunk ways I ever did here.

I looked around the room and saw the bottle. Sure enough it was super duper extra stench rum and ole Pooper hit half the bottle before he set into yankin' off that gal's toenail.

Now there's this other colored lady in the other examinatory room, and I peek in and see she plum nearly turned white. She's gettin' on up outta another one of them rocket man chairs and's gettin' into a sprint for the front Poop musta heard this, cause he came out and looked at his fancy fake watch he had on.

In fack she gets to runnin' out so fast she leaves her shoes on the floor.

Old Poop is sayin: "I gotta take a shit, I gotta take a shit. My time is valuable!" Then he runs on over to to the terlet. Five minutes later he comes out, and sez there'e someone he wants me to see. I say okey dokey on account that I'm there I'll just spend some of the time I had budgeted to visit ole Poop to try to offer some redeemin'. That's how these missions are done sometimes, you go and visit `em before they get damned.

The woman he just tortured is still cryin' but he don't pay her no mind. Nope, couldn't spare a minute. Oh well.

The gal in the other examinatory room was sittin there lookin' all flustered like she was waitin' for the sun to come up at midnight. I think that she was an eye tally ann on account Poop kept callin' her a ginny. Ginny this ginny that and: "Hey Crumb," he called me Crumb on account he couldn't remember my real name but that don't matter on account I don't particularly care for Doctor P, he IS a crumb and a half. So's I watch him get off that little stool in front of the doctor chair and there's theis little morsel on it. A shart. That's what the experts call `em. Comes from someone gotta go, gets a signal by way of their thinker brain and cuts a fart only there's surprise sampling uttered out of the tush. Hoowee that was a real stinkier. The lady'd who'd been waitin' for the sunrise looks at the stool on the stool and pukes.

Poop's already out the door headin' to the crapper again, and there I am stuck alone in a room with a pukey lady and a piece of poo on a little chair. I figure that I could either just run, or help this gal so I grab a bandage and wrap up her wound and say: "Don't mind old Poop he got hisself a stomack prollem and does dumb stuff."

Just as soon as I finish sayin' that, Poop sticks his head in the room, and looks at me like I'm the devil himself. He comes in and puts his hands on his hips and clamps his jaw, and looks at me like I just took his best fake watch.

The pukey gal reaches in her purse and pulls out a gun. Shee yatt.

She shot him right square in the gut and doody squirted out like that gusher up in Montana, only Old Faithul didn't smell like the innards of a day old dead gator. I had to leave.

Poop's time was up. I don't reckon he's goin' anyplace soon. Metaphysically speakin'-Hell don't have no toilet paper, and he'll be waitin' in purgatory, that holdin' area for the hellbound, for a spell till Satan figures out what to do with him.

This goes to show that some folks ain't got no redeemin' no matter how much time measurin' they do. It's what they done did with the time they got. Poop crapped his away.

Oh well.

The Incompetent Man
Trip's timely slant on Eustice's previous mission...

He had a chip on his shoulder. Actually some would say he had the whole forest resting on either side of his fat head and walked around daring the world to knock branch off. This guy carried not one, but two guns and kept a bullet chambered just in case he had to quick draw and fire-which, thank goodness he never did. He never did because he spent the last few decades in a haze of booze induced stupor barely making it though a day without a visit with the Captain, as in Morgan that is, he was a rummy. Yep, the Whateverologist of ill repute who knew-it-all could easily be picked out in a crowd by any one of many distinguishing features, foremost was his hunched posture, ashen skin, and perpetual grimace. This man used to stand a solid six feet and weighed in at a deuce and quarter. Nowdays he's about five ten and weighs in at a buck fifty, if that. Why? Booze, and lots and lots of it. This man can drink until he not only makes a fool of himself to the point where people refuse to speak with him after a dinner engagement, but insists that he's a genius-Yes. Rip Gazziss is a genius. In fact when he was younger and didn't drink rum, he drank wine-and did so by the gallon. He used to go through a box of Chateau Lafuck in two hours before going into a rant of meaningless drivel.

Rip. He had some very very serious gastrointestinal problems that resulted in surgery and having to wear an ostomy bag for a spell. But he still guzzled gallons of high powered juice.

This is a man who CAN NEVER BE WRONG. He has NO wiggle room for error, he refuses to admit that he does NOT know something, he's an expert after all, he is a specialist. Yeah, right.

He was a lazy drunk.

Who wakes up awaiting the moment that the first few drops of fluid hit his lips and the liquid trickles down his gullet to his stomach and explodes into the glow he's dreamed of. Then he's off to blackoutville and drunk calling and blathering, bickering, banter, and beat down bullying.

He was a mean drunk. There are some drunks that can just nod and pass out-not this guy, The belligerent sort who reminds you how smart he is and then berates, begrudges anyone and everyone who's in the world that isn't a trollish little man like himself. A guy who pissed away opportunities the way a race horse fills a jar after a run-He's what the public domain would use as a poster child-for a sixtyish man-as a stone cold loser-and a boozer.

A Dangerous Game: Diarrhea Roulette
Trip's curious journey into an unearthly underworld

There is a game played among the youth-actually all ages-of Americans these days which is not only dangerous, but it can get very stinky. It's a take off on Russian Roulette only played with laxatives. Think of the old movie, The Dear Hunter, and the scene where Christopher Walken has this bandana on his head at a table with a bunch of Vietnamese folks cheering and placing bets as to who's going to bust a cap in their head-there's one bullet in the gun-and they take turns pointing it at themselves and going...click. If they don't die, they win. Okay?

So you get a table of folks and a bottle of laxatives. There are maybe five or six people sitting at the table and the host lays out a couple pills in front of each player then puts a few rolls of toilet paper in the center. The first ones to grab the TP are out. As time passes, one by one grab a roll and run for the crapper. It can be pretty intense watching the faces of the players as they squirm with each burble or gurgle in the gut. After a spell the farting begins. Maybe a few sqeakers followed by a volley of long motorboating. The tension builds in the room-so does the stench-but bets are placed by the crowd as to who just might last out the others and the players get real edgy. Once in a while there's a blast followed by a player grimacing and saying: "Ew..." Which is usually a peanut in the underwear. Depending upon where the game's played a rectal sputter of feces is counted as a loss and the player excluded. The winner, usually the the most gaseous person at the table, is the one who doesn't grab the toilet paper and can hold it in the longest. Usually their skin's gone pale and they look like they may explode, but they DO hit the jackpot and when they hit, they hit big.

The underground games are played throughout most cities and usually the building needs to be condemned after a game, but after you've seen it played once, you're hooked. In fact, you might just want to play. I'd skip the refried beans and Mexican meal or a tofu, veggie supremo meal, but some of us can't resist the challenge. I know because I played in a championship match last month. Eustice was tight with funds. He didn't approve of *any* sort of gambling, and after all, I *did* leave Vegas to work with him. Whatever, there was one situation that made me lay off the game, and maybe run it by the chief of Soul Saving, but then again, some things are better left as they are. I got away from that crowd because of Buck Buttsqueeze, a man definitely with little if any redeeming qualities.

Buck `Buttsqueeze' McCroy held the title for longest post Senna stool saver and the great Minnie `Mystool' Koplman a close second. I sat down at the table where a ceiling fan spun slowly overhead. I had on a white shirt, pair of khakis and headband. I wore Rayban Wayfarer shades so no one could see my eyes bulge-which they would-if I got a really bad toilet itch. So the host lays out the lax, that's what they call it: laying out the lax, or lol, and I take mine and wait. There are two other players at the table, amateurs who I figured were in on it as a lark of sorts Me? I was in it for the glory, the grandness of the game, and of course the money. The pot was big, not like the one the loose stooled losers would be squatting on, it was some serious coin. I waited. The crowd began to grow. There were all sorts of folks in the audience, many very well dressed as if they were at some grand sporting event or polo match or maybe coming form an opera. Let me share this with you, they were in for a real symphony today because within an hour the other players were screeching, sputtering and making sounds no human I thought capable of and, they were all under the table. The host had lit candles to consume the smells, but it didn't do much because I could see the eyes of people in the room begin to water as the anal orchestrations ramped up. Things settled down into a lull of a sputter here a blast there, but nothing so outrageous that 911 had to be called, until....McCroy let loose an unearthly tuba-like haroomph which lasted for more than thirty seconds and hit notes only a maestro could aspire to. In fact the rivitting sounded like a 1957 Chevy whose muffler had fallen off and the deep bass rumbling nearly knocked one of the rookies out cold. The exhaust was wicked and the candles glowed brightly only to finally dim down as the gas mixed with the room's air. One of the rookies snatched a roll of TP and darted toward the can. I sat bravely, feeling a slight urge myself, but the tenesmus passed.

Minnie 'Mystool' must have had some feminist inclinations because she shouted out: "Hey, let's up the ante, give me another round."

Mighty Casey was at bat. I said, go on, and popped another pair of Sennas. Another newbie took his toilet paper and called it quits or something that rhymes with that. He was gone and it was just Mcroy, Minnie, another strange greenish face, and me. We waited.

An hour passed and the host was working the room like a whore working an aircraft carrier's crew making the rounds before the fleet left town, taking bets who'd be the last man, or woman, holding on. I played it cool despite urgings from below.

BOOM! McCroy let loose another blast, this wasn't some tuba burst, it was a the real McDoody! Shit, he'd farted a peanut. Damn, the look on his face was complete despair-he'd lost by default. Minnie smiled and then narrowed her eyes and leaned toward me: "You're next, pal," she said.

So it was the three of us. The rookie, Minnie and me. Only now I figured out that the rookie wasn't just a rookie at all, he was the world champion long distance stool saver, Nick Jabrone. He had the land speed record for the fifty yard dash to the toilet in twelve countries and had won ten hot dog eating contests in a three day period without nearly a belch. He leaned back in his chair and slowly shook his head from side to side as if he knew he'd take the pot, which grew with each passage of wind.

By now, the host had donned a World War I era gas mask, I think it was largely for effect because the crowd started laughing and raising the ante. And the crowd, the looks on their faces. Like poo was in the air. And it was.

I don't know what happened next, but all hell broke loose and the place was surrounded by a hazmat team in those special suits hosing the joint down. I was taken into custody and placed in an isolation cell. I don't particularly blame them.

Minnie, from what I understand exploded, blinding twelve people in the audience and deafening two. Although the injuries were temporary I would have went on trial for reckless release and aiding and abetting and my lawyer, thanks to Eustice, plead the case out because I was willing to turn State's evidence-It was bogus laxatives from China. I learned something from that experience. Use your own bathroom, and never fart in public.

Seeney was beginning to watch me carefully thinking I may have slipped into Satan's wicked ways...again.

Just Another Morning for John Q

Trip's trouble's follow him like a vapor trail from a jetliner, or a case of bad gas...

I didn't set my alarm clock because I don't have one. Not in this place. No more haunted houses for me, after that last freebie. No way. So I awoke with a jolt to disturbing noise.

There is banging on the door of my new apartment and it wasn't the friendly tap tap tapping of Eustice to remind me I was late for work at the Center. I ignored it for a few minutes, and reflected on the day ahead, and dozed off. I don't know how much time passed but fell into a deep sleep. A loud rat-tat-tat, awoke me from a marvelous dreamscape where all things flowed in a soft porn pleasurable haze. I sat up, resting myself on elbows and the dream's imagery faded with each volley of knocks. It sounded too serious to respond to, especially at this unearthly hour before the sun poked above the horizon.

The woman in bed with me snored softly and I pulled the sheet up to cover her bare porcelain shoulders, pausing to let my gaze linger on the way her dark hair fell across her smooth skin and very innocent face. I tiptoed over to the window overlooking the parking lot and nudged the curtain a bit to see if it was the cops. Always the first thought, if it was a fire or some terror attack, alarms would ahooga many decibels above the persistent pounding at my front door.

I slipped on some jeans and walked barefoot over to the front door considering a look through the peephole, but recalled seeing a movie about someone who had their eye put out by an ice pick by some crazed zombie. But zombies wouldn't have made it past the security desk, hell-they wouldn't have let anyone in short of a cop or court appointed process server....And that's when it hit me.

My heart raced as the adrenaline pulsed fast and hard making my fingers numb and that crappy rush that feels like too much coffee and too little sleep. Boom booom boom, I'd just zipped up my fly and looked out another window-sure enough a Crown Vic was parked in a no-parking spot three floors down. The security guard must have given the person at the door a nod and a smile after seeing some court appointed document and ID-The car could've been cop, but judging by the lack of identification as such and the decal in the right corner of the car's windshield figured it to be the vehicle of a PS, process server-a court appointed deliver yman of bad news.

Vegas found me. Some markders called in, and my bad days were catching up with me. A subpeona awaited, and it probably had my name on it. And it, was on the other side of the door and that'd mean a day of phone calls, finding a lawyer to raise reasonable defenses and worst of all having to be somewhere at some given time to face a judge. I'm not one to be anywhere at any given time for any reason unless it's on my terms. And the terms of the life I chose were such that doing so-being in a courtroom-weren't in the cards, not now, not today, not ever. I had to dodge the rat bastard. The rules of the game, oh it's a game all right, are that the PS has 120 days to serve process on a party or the judge dismisses it and the lawsuit is dismissed without prejudice, which means that they can refile but that ain't cheap, sometimes the prick suing you petitions the court for an enlargement of time, they usually get another 120 days, so far this this'd be the 600th day.

They, the casionos, and the old gambling debt I racked up, wanted my ass in court. They used to just break your thumbs, but now they're civilized. Oh they'll get me somehow, but here's the rub with that-I'm not even an American citizen, but for those who are, they probably swing things like this along these lines, Meet John Q Public:

Oh, I'm sorry I didn't introduce myself-my name's Q. John Q Public-they guy they write about in the newspapers, well if they still had newspapers, the guy they say all American citizens are your average Joe. Someone up to their ears in debt, crummy job, miserable week to week existence paying bills to get deeper and deeper in debt and drinking 2.5 alcoholic beverages per day, 35-45 year age group, male, divorced, professional living in a so-called ordinary middle class neighborhood driving a so-called middle class car. Yep, that's me, a regular regular guy. Go on ask the folks over at the gas station, I use regular. Ask my doc-if I had one-I don't have health insurance and if I did, I wouldn't see a doc anyways, I'd see some nurse practitioner or physician's assistant or hell, wait till I was so sick they'd rush me to the hospital. Then again, who really rushes anyone that's an average Joe anywhere? They'd probably idle the ambulance to the nearest charity dump and roll the gurney into the lobby to wait for ten hours along with rest of humanity.

Boom boom boom. There's the PS again, Vegas calling, they don't just leave without lingering and banging on account in this county, Palm Beach, Florida, process servers get paid to hand those papers to the subject-You have to actually need to have a face-to-face, the PS has to physically place the papers in your hand after you've been named by name and identified as the person on the document, the lawsuit that's been filed cost whoever's suing you about five hundred bucks in legal fees and you gotta figure another thou to retain counsel to take the case and work it through the system. Oh I've been through this before in Las Vegas, and once you're on the books you can forget about dropping off the radar until they find out you aren't even an American.

Boom boom booom. Tenacious little bastard, huh? I was just thinking these things when my gal came out of the bedroom, the blankets bunched up covering her breasts, eyes wide open.

"Process server?" She shrugged.

"Yeah," I held up a finger to my lips.

"You want me to do the blow-off?" She said.

"I don't know. The place is rented out in a fugazzi name, but the car, that's legit, the PS probably scoped out the parking lot and saw it, figured I was here."

"I could pull the borrowed car routine, tell him that I haven't seen you in a month, you're living in Miami and you're a rat bastard routine-Usually works." She said in that annoyed tone that women have when they haven't had enough sleep.

"I've pulled that too many times. This one," I hitched my thumb toward the door, "is probably a PS who's done some scoping out at the Soul Salvation Center, and knows where I am. Fucking Eustice."

"Let's just go back to bed and say fuck `em."

"Yeah." She said. "We could do that," and pulled the blankets up.

So we did. Fuck `em.

An hour later I got up to take a leak. For the hell of it figured I'd take a look out the window. I'd be a liar if I said the sudden arrival of a process server didn't rankle me. How could they know I was here? I'm an Australian citizen who's been living in Vegas...

AT THE GROCERY STORE
Trip's Day Before Tomorrow

I knew my past was catching up with me. Maybe some old markers in Vegas were being called in, or I was being warned in some karmic way that my work with Seeney was off-kilter. Maybe the constellation of weirdness was coincidence, then again maybe not. I generally tend not to believe in coincidences, and tried to get my mind off of the possibility my involvement with Seeney might have some higher otherworldly origins. I take solace and blow off steam milling around grocery stores. So that's where I headed. I made sure the coast was clear no one on my tail. I stop at lights, wait a few beats, eyes always in the mirrors. I take the back streets often making constant right turns forming a circle, so if anyone was following me, I would know. Who else would drive around in circles before heading toward thier deistination? I was satisfied none of the old demons, or newly developed ones were around, found a grocery store in a nice neighborhod, parked, and headed into the store. Maybe try and have some fun. Fun...it's been a while.

So I'm over at the grocery store fetchin' some dog food for Zip the wonder dog. I got this big ole bag of Purina on the conveyor belt and the lady behind me, not exactly a pin-up gal for Victoria's Secret, more along the lines of Field and Stream in that large around the aisle

sort of way. I guess she was tryin' to be cute and bein' chatty. She giggled and said: "Is that for your dog?" I look on over at her and see that she's waiting for an answer. I say to myself: Damn that's either one dumb schtarker or she's hittin' on me. "No ma'am, that's for me. I'm on the dog food diet. Dropped fifty pounds on it, two weeks," and snapped my fingers. "And you're good to go."
"Really? It looks like it tastes horrible...but if it works-I've tried all sorts of diets," she said. "Tell me more."

Shit, I say to myself can people really be this friggin' dumb?"

"You put a handful in you pocket and take a few pieces out and chew on them throughout the day.
Whenever you feel hungry, you pop a few and after a while it starts to really taste good." I pointed at the bag's ingredients and said, "Check it out, all natural, everything you need to be healthy, bright eyes, great fur, good bones, the whole shebang." By now the clerk's scratching his head and the guy behind her in line is busting up laughing. I wait a few beats and say: "I landed myself in the hospital."

"Go on," she said. "Really?"

"Intensive care, tubes out of every orifice, IVs in both arms. A real wreck." I said softly.

She got all serious and leans toward me, "From the dog food diet and you're doing it again?"

"No, I stepped off the curb to sniff a poodles butt."

And then she hurled her purse at my gut and I barfed on her. I left without the dog food.

Zip was still hungry

So I go to another grocery store and put some dog food, a can of tuna and some frozen corn on the conveyor belt. I'm standing in line and the lady ahead of me, maybe in her seventies looks at me and says, "Sonny you look so familiar."

"Me?" I said.

"No. No. You look just like my son. He died last year." She goes into fumbling in her purse and yanks out a photo. "Here's his picture."

I look at the pic and there's an oriental guy about ten years older than me. He doesn't look anything at all like me. I say, "That's nice ma'am."

"Sir, could you please do me this small favor?"

"What would that be?" Cheesh, I figure whatever it is to be a short con or some other scam.

"Would you just call me `Ma' like you mean it, just once?"

"Lady, I just want to go home and feed my dog."

"Please, please do this. It's the anniversary of his passing and it would mean so much to me." And she starts to cry.

The line's getting longer and I say to myself, what the hey? "Okay lady. Here you go....Ma,"

"Thank you," she said, gathering her grocery bag and walking out of the store.

Good riddance, I say to myself and she stops right there at the door and shouts out, "Goodbye son."

"Goodybye," I said. But she's not moving, she's prodding me with her hand. Finally I say, "Ma."
And she leaves.

The clerk rings up Zip's dinner, my tuna and corn and says: "That'll be three hundred forty six dollars and twelve cents."

"What?" I said. "I've only got a few items here."

"Your mother said that you'd be picking up the tab. She IS your mother, I heard her call you `son' and you call her `Ma'...Debit, Credit or Cash?"

I pay the guy and rush out to the parking lot and the old broad's getting into her friggin' ride-a Rolls Royce. I see the door's open and drop my shit and run over to the car. I see her leg's dangling out the door and dive toward it and grab it and squeeze. She's screaming and honking the horn. I'm pullin' and pullin' and I'm pullin' your leg too. I don't have a dog. But I do have this nifty Rolls Royce with an old lady with a picture of an Oriental guy in her bag-she's in the trunk. It's a nice driving car.

IF SOMETHING DOESN'T POPULATE THE SCREEN...*Is it real?*

They were the times of random growth and confusion, America built upon itself with borrowed money on borrowed time, but everyone at least had a shot at the dream. And that's what it was-a chimera of sorts, some extraordinary period when all grand things-and things they were-could be owned, purchased and fondled with the presentation of a credit card. A war on drugs raged on every border and within, a war on crime, a war on one thing or another largely soldiered by flailing armies of well insured troupers jumping in to save the streets from crime and mayhem which oddly failed before it began and then they came, conquered and over ran an age ripe with disposable income, addled minds and freewheelery-they came, they developed, they permutated and conquered-the machines. The meltdownof `o8 was the beginning of a new terrain and the all became small and lived only as it populated a Monster glass screen. The downfall of mindless youth did not start with drugs, alcohol and sex-it could have-but the first video game, the first high resolution screen, the first Tweet, Facebook friend signaled the electronic vectors that wiped out any social skill before it became an extinct behavior before the first log on-it was over and the age of idiocy was upon the world.

And with that preamble a rather protracted rant, Les Grummer went over to the Sport's Super Senter to fetch himself a new pair of swimming goggles. Les, a swimmer and athlete of sorts needed some gear and the SSS was the prime location for discount goods including but not at all limited to the modest of mod jogging attire, swiftest designer shoes for running in the rain, rivetting racqketball, squash and tennis tools with the latest and greatest pro endorsed symbols signs and signatures-Yep the game was the equipment and if you had a Tiger Woods endorsed set of golf clubs your putter would bang a hole-in-one every time you left the fairway, even if your fairway was a woman and the woman was your wife-but Les stayed at his own clubhouse and wasn't a golfer. He just wanted a new pair of goggles and maybe a swimsuit. He had that sense of insouciance Captain Kirk must've had upon entering the bridge on the Starship Enterprise when the doors slid open with an audible pfft and pneumatic thump without his touching thing. They slid shut behind him and the gal at the counter didn't raise her head from her new iSomething that'd been the focus of her attention. Two customers waited to check out but that'd have to wait. Rihanna had to text her gal pal about the new Lady Gag yourself video and didn't have time for silly customers. But Les being Les rapped his knuckles on the counter and said: "Hey where's the goggles," to the texting teen.

She ignored him, holding up a finger for flash and getting back to her QWERTYing. A foot tapping customer let her merchandise set on the counter and exchanged a brief: `Kids these days' glance with Grummer and left her overpriced sweathshirt on the counter.

"Hey kid, is there a manager here," Les said with some authority. He'd gotten up in her face and stood inches from the young woman, who finally averted her gaze from her cell-phone, mini-computer, be all, end all and love of her life and stared at this 40ish man who was leaning over the counter.

"Sir, you'll have to step back." She took a step back and stumbled bumping her over French fied butt on the adjacent counter. "I'm going to have to call my manager," and she picked up a phone, pressed pair of buttons and the loudspeakers echoed througout the store.

Within a minute a tall, overly pimply faced man-boy stood in front of Les Grummer, who turned to face him. One of the customers waiting in line would later recall zit face as having the expression that looked like a leg cramp as he scowled at the customer, who, for goodness sakes had the audacity to not take his place in line, hurry up and wait and ask to divert the manager from the difficult duties of doing nothing-actually he was playing on his X-Box but didn't want to put it on pause, but that's a different story. But he was a full foot taller than Grummer and introduced himself as: "I'm Brock Denton, manager of SSS how can I help you," with the tone reserved for petty tyrants universally. He didn't extend a hand to shake, rather balled up his fists and placed them on his hips in the defiant way people pretending to have something better to do often do-All this without, Les would surmise without an acting class too. After all, a zit faced kid not more than 25, not in college and the verbal skills of a chipmunk must have done a good two years working the floors to make it to the lofty title as `Store Manager' and his neato orange polyester vest sealed the deal with the word `Store Manager' emroidered above his right nipple.

He thumped his chest after a long silence hung between them like a soggy enchilada from the Taco Bell across the street, which, Les would describe as pretty much the essence of the young chap's body odor. Working those video game buttons can really set off the vapors.

"Listen, Chip," Les said reading his name, which wasn't embroidered, it was on a plastic name tag-suggesting this was a new position for the kid-that store managers were interchangable and that the position held today may not be there tomorrow. "I bought these goggles two weeks ago and they're falling apart." Les lied.

Les was a good liar, he'd managed to bullshit his way through more arduous situations involving much more intricate and complex transactions but this was too easy to resist.

Chip inspected the goggles in that peek-a-boo manner reserved for quick glances of a discarded food wrapper and said, without preamble: "If you purchased the extended warrantee for them, you can swap them out for a new pair."

Extended freaking warrantee for a pair of el-cheapo swim goggles? Holy crap, what has the insurance industry come to, insuring a less than twenty dollar item for what?

"Chip, Chipper, Chipowski, my good man," Les said, in his slickest most friendly bro-like tone. "Do you know how crazy it is to buy a warantyon crummy plastic googles is?"

To which Chip replied, "Sir, if you're going to become difficult I'm going to have to ask you to leave." He fists had whitened from the pressure he'd built up from digging them into his hips and the leg cramp face went crimson.

"Hey relax."

"The name is Chip." He thumped his chest.

"Okay Chip I just need to know where the swim goggles are and I'll pay twenty bucks for new pair."

Chip looked over at the teeny bopper on line and asked and aswered before she could avert her gaze from Facebook friends: "When was that sales meeting? Oh three minutes?" He lifted one of his pink knuckles raised it to his eyes and looked at an imaginary watch. "I have a meeting but can take you over to goggle area."

Les did, pointed to a department, stood at the rows and rows of goggles and said: "Next time get the warranty. I have to get to a meeting." Which Les presumed was code for I got to get back to my video game or go jerk off to the internet porn on account I am on the clock.

"Thanks Chip," Les said.

He found the most expensive goggles there and took them out of the container and tried them on. They fit just swell. When he took them, to the texting teen she stared at him as if he missed the parade and stepped on chewing gum that needed to be scraped off his shoes but didn't want to remind him that it'd be a mess. "Do you have a container?"

"No," Les lied.

She took the goggles, scanned them with a pistol-like device again and again and stared at the computer screen checkout device finally letting out a gush of frustration. "This isn't scanning. There's no record of this on the computer."

Les shrugged. "It must be on the computer along with the price. Why don't you call the manager, Chip?"

"He's in a meeting. This doesn't populate the screen. You'll have to wait. I have other customers."

"Ma'am, I don't have all day, the manger pointed these out to me, remember, it was two minutes ago you called him and he took me over to the goggle department?"

"Oh yeah, Chip, the goggles, you talked to the manager and the item isn't on the screen. How much were they?"

"The manager said I could help myself on account there was no packaging."

She had a look on her face that could have stopped a stalker dead in his fantasy. "No packaging, not in the computer. I guess if it isn't on the screen it doesn't exist in our store." She said.

Les stared at her and shurgged again. "I guess not." The dumb kid actually said that.

She preceded to put the goggles in a huge plastic bag and a coupon sheet the size of this week's People Magazine and fake-smiled. "Have a nice day."

Les looked at her and wondered if there was a statute of limitations on stupid. Deciding that there wasn't he smiled back and said, "Thanks."

"Are you sure you don't want a warranty?"

The Star Trek doors slid shut as Les strolled with his new goggles out into the maze of cars in the parking lot with his goggles.

Velcro: Another Brilliant Gush of Wind

It is melancholy truth that dreams fade. In fact even a happy dream where you're laughin' in your sleep goes away and you're bustin' a gut so hard it makes your collsarn eyes go into waterin' but all you got when you awake is tear streaks and can't recall what was so funny. Why'm I sayin' this just the way I do right now? That there's a right good question on account a couple days ago me and my cousin Jep went on over to fetch us a pair of new shoes. This wasn't just a hop over to the mall-nope. Not with cousin Jep, for him to go shoppin' it had to be epic. That meant some weird road trip. What the hey? I didn't have anything better doin' -nothin' at all. Mind you, I wouldn't start off spinnin' a yarn unless there was a good reason for it. Yep a good reason indeed, Yep, a pair of those fine nicely padded, corn conformin'. springy bouncin' shiny colored, easy to tie fancy jogger's shoes. I ain't had me no new shoes since the economy went crummy and figured that I'd do right fine with the kicks I had-and good ones they are-but cowboy boots only go so far when you're walkin' down the beach. And Jep? Well he was drivin' a car that was sort of borrowed-that's what he said-but I figure he just forgot to tell the fella he borrowed it from he took it. So Jep, he sort of conned me into takin' a road trip on down to the Sunshine State itself, which, on its surface sounded right fine on account where I come from the leaves done fell off the trees and the sky looked like a big ole quilt of gloom that you couldn't poke through with even the mightiest fireworks. So I said: Sure. And we got ourselves all liquored up and head out on the highway. Don't go askin' me no details on account by the time we hit the state line my gums were stuck to my teeth and my tongue had grown fur on it. Jep says I blacked out, but I don't think so on account my skin was still it's usual leathery parchment tone it's always been and I do rememmer havin' a strange dream.

The dream went somethin like this:

I was slidin' on the ice. I mean like at a hockey rink or the place they got the Ice Capades but there weren't no pansies dancin' around with ice skates and sissified tights on twirlin' to Elton John and spotlights gleamin'. Nope. Just some big machine that made ice. I think it was called a Zamboni or somethin' like that. Well there I was in this narrow tunnel and just like that WHOOSH-some big blast of air pushes me forward on out onto the ice. I go into slidin' and slidin' hard and fast. I try slowin' down the skid and go all skit skat and skiddly bob te bo-like that guy from the Popeye cartoons I usually watch while I'm eatin' breakfast. But this is real serious, I mean real serious on account I ain't got no control over stuff and I'm on my tush and slidin' fast and I don't know wheres I'm headed and I get this sense like I'm gonna crash-I mean intensive care broken bone-crash into somethin' and somethin' hard too. It gets me this thought in my head like I gotta do somethin' and I look at my hands. My fingers are pink nubs. I know I said I got leathery like skin, but my fingers is different and I let `em get to bein' soft on account it's been a spell since I done did anything that'd grow a callus on them like play my guitar-I used to be a real rocker-but that ended when one string or another got busted. But I'm goin' faster and faster and stop lookin' at those pink nubs and the scenery on my right and left is turnin' into a blur and instead of slowin' down I'm speedin' up headin' toward somethin' it's somethin fierce, I know it, I know it for certain so I just dig my fingers into the ice. HOOWEEE it hurts...I can see ice slush fly up on the sides and make a big ole feathery wake of white mush curtain and hear the sounds of fingernails on a goopy chalkboard like a thousand cats screamin' out in a fight over a piece of Sockeye salmon. Next thing I know that white curtain of slush turns red and my fingers are screamin on up my pain circuits to my thinker brain and it hurts like a sumbitch stuck a firecracker up my bunghole and set it afire! I look down and see my fingers and the skin's gone and their worn on down to my finger bones and then the bones they's turned into birds feet, no, they're bigger and I'm startin' to slow down and they're gettin a grip, they're dug into the ice and they're dug in hard and they stop me like a brick wall. I go flyin' over my hands and I'm on my back lookin' forward at my fingers-SHEEYATT I GOT TIGER CLAW HANDS!

And then I stand up and look and stare at my hands and I'm like this big ole jungle cat, a tiger and I get to feelin' real powerful and I can do anything. I am the master of my destiny. I get to lookin' around the rink and shakin' my head like I am the coolest locust in the swarm and a real leader of leaders and start struttin' toward that narrow hall I come in at and all of a sudden there's this tap on my left shoulder. Sheeyattt....I turn around and it's the guy drivin' the Zamboni-he decks me and my knees crumple and fall flat on my face.

Next thing I know cousin Jep's shakin' me. "Wake up dummy wake up. We're almost in Florida. We're gonna get us some new shoes."

Sheeyatt. I look at my fingers and say to myself it ain't gonna happen on account they're all shredded up and bloody. What the heck? How'm I gonna tie them.

Jep leans over and narrows his eyes and shakes his head and says: "Velcro dummy, fucking Velcro."

MISSION #666: SPOOKDICULOUS
The Dreams We Cherish

Doc Wiley said I was a dreamer and there was no way I could save folks souls. He said that lots of people believed that, and said: The dreams we cherish are the ones we're least wantin'to wake from. Or somethin' like that.

I didn't reckon nothin' I had been dreamin' but for nothin', and admit that comment got me riled. Hellsfire. I had a callin', and even if folks thought it was livin' in a dream, so be it. I didn't right know if what I was gonna do next was gonna take that notion to the next level and that the dream, so to speak just might be over. Why? Well, this is what happened: I go over to mah office over at the Soul Salvition Center, and on my desk I saw a note from Doc Wiley. It wasn't like him to leave notes, and the way it was writ didn't look like his scrawl. But bein' the respectin' guy I am, figured it right to stick to Trip's request. The note said to meet him out in the Everglades...hmm. Now let me tell you, as a man who'd come face to face with the eternal and stared down Satan himself there was somethin' altogether unwholesome goin' on-felt it in my bones. Meet Trip Wiley out in the middle of noplace? I knew then that there was more to this than any other mission. At the moment I had a sense like all the pieces of a cosmic puzzle fell into place, and that this was a mission I had to take on alone. I could hear my heartbeat like the bass part from Roundabout by Yes. Somethin' real serious is gonna go down, and I got things right prepared in case it went down funky.

I took a look around the Center, did what I had to, and mounted up. I chose my lucky hat, tied my bandana, and put on and extra pair of underwear...you never know when you might need `em.

KNOCKOUT WHAM BAM OH NO MA'AM

She hailed, so it would at some later time be recalled from a place Eustice knew as Scorneo. This section of hell was a compartment in Hades, several sections away from the stadiums which housed those with poor credit scores. Scorneo was akin to a coliseum of sorts, a place others described to be similar in the wailing sounds as the straits Odysseus traversed where the scorned women bemoaned their adulterous spouse, and for one reason or another committed some earthly behavior reaching some threshold worthy of damnation. Because these women's brash, venomous blather was so rivettingly heinous, Satan himself declared a special section of hell to be off-limits by his minions, and named it Scorneo and the offical language was called Zanenna.

Hence the chatter among those women of Scorneo were referred to talking the language known as Zanenna Talk. A barritone murmur of foul damning hatred for all things masculine, and a particular disdain for the slender female form in all her perkiness.

It was said that for sport, some of Satan's minions would toss a men's magazine depicting lovely-by earthly accounts-young scantily clad women into the Den of Scorn, a gathering place of sorts were the repetitive rants of scorned women played like a scratched vinyl record with a bent stylus on an ancient record player the same song over and over until the hell birds fell from the sky, and all of Hades could hear the wail of the collective Zanenna songs. Upon the dropping of a "girly" magazine the scorned women would collectively seize in an orhestra of shrill vomit worthy reverberations that some minions would actually lose consciousness. Eustice said:" They'd plum up and die if they weren't already dead." Seeney described these women as "she-beasts ravaged by their anger they resembled tattered pit bulls, who'd shred the pin up's and stomp their feet like cloven hoofed heifers until the very ground of Hades rumbled."

Satan, it was rumored, enjoyed the sound, and despite scuttlebut to the contrary kept up his subscriptions to several magazines, never in fact, according to earthly publishers, to have failed to renew but for an economic slump during the Carter years.

As the message suggested, Eustice Seeney was to meet a new client at a remote location. Even Seeney was suspicious as the locale was smack dab in the Everglades accesible only by airboat. Directly, he would recall from his youth as a tour guide giving airboat rides in the middle of nowhere.

This location was indeed at a crossroads between several large bodies of water, both inhabited by vicous, hungry sea beasts, and the great swamp, the Everglades, brimming with hungry alligators. As such this provided for complete isolation, and in the event of casualties the Everglades has made for a marvelous place to dump a body.

Unaware of who or why this meeting was arranged Eustice, unable to reach any of his colleagues, cohorts, or confederates knew one thing for sure. He would be attending this meeting alone, and he knew for certain one thing, that if things did not go well: there would be no prisoners.

SWAMP THINGS

The Florida Everglades is a river of sawgrass, gators, and sub tropical warm water, mostly fresh, often brakish and always alive with all the critters you'd hate to wake up in bed with. You sure's hell wouldn't want to be stuck in that swamp, not for all the winnings at one of the Seminole Casino's skirting the swamp's periphery. But there it is, this grand aquafir that sets at the southern third of the state as prehistorically unscathed as some of the creatures who make this unique piece of the planet their home. Human, and reptile, avian and insect can be found often not to your liking if you're truly unprepared, but then again, who is ever prepred for the mysteries which lurk in this grand swamp?

A small mound the size of a baseball diamond somewhere smack dab in the dead center of who knew where stuck out like a bloody nose on an albino. Eustice saw it from the airboat he'd been motoring for the last hour from up north near the Loxahatchee docks. He knew the terrrain as well as one could, but no one knew it with any great precision. The ever changing currents from the Atlantic Ocean and Gulf of Mexico combined with hundreds of streams and creeks criss crossed the five million acre watershed blanketing this part of the Florida Peninsula. Finally he saw it, he'd followed the instructions and double checked his GPS-there it was...the meeting place.

He throttled back and let the huge fan on the airboat idle and drifted to the mound's bank where he could make out a gathering of people. Oddly he thought there were no other boats, and he wondered how they got there.

At the moment the aluminum hull touched the shore a rumble from above seemed to cause tiny rivulets to appear in the water, and blades of sawgrass stir. From above it would appear as a river of grass swaying from the whump whump whump of a hellicopter but, there was no helicopter, just the drum beats of an angering sky. What was this place, and why here, why now, and what for? Eustice Seeney the man who'd been to hell felt a fear that crept slowly up from a place he'd felt before and knew what lay beyond could be more dire than hell itself.

Eustice shut down the engine and left the airboat. It's hull was halfway ashore, and he gave it a little tug to make sure it wouldn't float off. It seemed fine, what was awaiting him made him shudder, but despite his uneasy sense that something was awry he righted himself, and equipped solely with his wits forged on to an uncertain meeting.

HARIDANDELION AIN'T NO FLOWER
And a Broom Ride to the Tomb...

Hoowee, she was a meanderin' monster from the highway of haridans who'd flown in on a broomstick from some witchy place, and I tweren't quite sure it was hell. After all last time I seen her she was livin'-sort of. Collsarn it I knew that beeyatch and I didn't right like her when I done first met her.

Well there she was, short squat and like one of them beetles from an ancient Egyptian Tomb, only instead of an exoskeleton like a bug she had pasty white fleshs that was all wrinkly and had a pair of breastesses the size of watermelons so stale and soggy they drooped beneath her big ole waist. I walked toward her, and saw her narrow beady eyes sunk deep in that puffy face that looked like it was made of cookie dough. He lips were as thin as pipe cleaners, and the top one just as fuzzy. She looked like she could ward off boners like sack of saltpeter.

I done met this woman some time ago. She's the lady who chopped off her boy's penis, and turned the the other one full blown homo, even planned up a big ole gay wedddin' -Yep the groom of the groom chickened out at the last minute on account her boy'd taken to the drugs and spent more time in rehab than a fella with half his guts does on the crapper. Hoowee, I was supposed to set this ole she beast on a path toward righteousness, and forgot how hopeless it'd be. She done went and hid the homo drug boy under the bed for deserten' from the army. That was a major blow up, or I should say he done blew a major, and then a general and the whole shebang turned out as sour as truckload of lemons.

That boy'd be cleanin' glory holes for all time. And the other kid, the one she got all ferbidgitty about his manliness? Hells fire, she done took up with some lesbians and got this macho fella into believin' he was secretly a gal! She done begged, borrowed and stole to get his payoonis hacked off at some chop shop in Shanghai, and the lesbo cohorts? Hellsfire, when I found out they was con artists the fuzzy lipped haridan went apeshit and threatened to have me killed. So much for that mission...I barely escaped with mah life. Turned out she hated her ex husband so much that she'd be willin' to do anything to get even so took to punishin' her chillin' to settle a score that can't be settled. I tried to tell her, but I reckon John Q stepped in, and she was facin' some real jail time. I reckon her ex hubby married that skinny model lookin' gal and did more fuckin' than a pair of horn dogs hopped up on jimsatical Kama Sutras or somethin' like that...

"Or something like that."

Where the hell'd that voice come from? It was a deep murmur-some spooky hibbidy jibbidy all encompassin' sound system she must've installed in the burshes or somethin'-I looked but didn't see but for nothin' but for a few gators that'd crawled on up next to her. No, it was her, and she had some kinda wicked womanly words that were somehow cosmicly amplified by the big feminist floor show of Frisco-I say that cause when I went to track down the dickless boy, he was livin' in San Fancisco, home of the homeos-I know I know it ain't politically correct, but when you're in the middle of noplace and ain't nobody around but some real scary lady you done pissed off I mizewell a been O.J. Because there was no dream team to get me off-I could see it in those eyes she got me out here for one reason, and just like she wanted to do to that ex hubby, she wanted me dead, and them gators was lookin' hungry.

I looked at her just as another series of thunder went to rumble, and clouds filled the sky so fast I thought they was gator farts gone skyward....Lightning catappulted among the clouds, I stared for second then back at the haridan, she had a gun and it was pointed right at my head.

"You won't have a corpse this time Seeney. This time you'll stay in hell...for all eternity." She laughed.

Her laugh was mirthless, a strained series of sounds as authentic and out ouf place as bagpipes at a Bar Mitzvah. There was no joy between the two people on this remote plot of land in that sea of transient mounds, which with a change in the wind, a quirk of the tides be gone within days, maybe hours.

Eustice stood his ground, and waited. Finally he set his jaw, clenched his fists, and was about to as what the hell this was about. He was just ready to uter his first words when the sky opened up forming a dark chasm, like a gap opening into some grand nothingness that blacked out the world in its entirety.

And in a flash, everyone that Eustice ever met, crossed paths with, stood forming a circle of what Seeney would call a grand squaring off. The sky closed, but the clouds remained and the murmur of thunder continued. The crowd of people began to chant, and to Eustice they looked like a gathering of zombies, none of them, even the folks he'd been friendly with seemed marble eyed, and set on one thing-the end of Eustice Seeney.

Even Trip Wiley seemed like a Stepford creep ready to do whatever he was going to do along with the crowd. To Eustice, it didn't look promising. He may have made a grave error making the trip alone.

The Sky's Gone Plum Zooey

IT HAPPENED THIS WAY FOLKS
...and wasn't what I'd expected at all at all, lisen:

I swear's that I was at some divine intervention. I got suckered into coming out into the swamp so all these folks could cajole me into one collsarn thing or another....and seein' as how I ain't got nothin' to give a hoot about, figure the only place they wanna put me in'd be a looney bin. I don't reckon there's a rehab for the damned, or some twelve steps out of hell program. Hell no. Of course there was that Dante guy who write that book about all the layers of Hades, but this? This obscene gathering of folks was gonna do somethin' fierce. I knew I had only one smart thing to do, and that was run.... run run run, as fast as my legs'd carry me.

I got over to the airboat, cranked up the big ole fan and throtteled it up. I looked over my shoulder and saw the intervention maniac robot zombies move like they were fixin' to do somethin'. Just as my rig was far enough away I caught sight of of `em and it'd make any fellas nose hair fall out. They broke into a dance like they was some Las Vegas showgirls, only real frumpy. It was some horid middle of the Everglades hoochey coo dance.

The airboat's wake stirred the hungry gator's, sendin' 'em off balance for a spell, and then somethin' happened. The whole earth felt like it shifted on its axis, and all of everything changed. I didn't have me but a clue what it was.

I'd seen big storms, tornados, hurricanes, and a bunch of stuff, but this was some cosmic hoodoo. Maybe that dance conjured up some spirits. The pressure dropped, and I could hear a high pitched sound like sirens goin' off, and a series of lghtning bolts catapulted across the sky like one of them science experiment machines with the big balls. Some electrostatic thingamajig went to churnin', and the wind picked up. A cyclone went to spinnin' and everyone, the dancers, the gators, and me too. We was caught up in it, and like in that Wizard of Oz movie, everyone was bein' spun around and around. It all happened so fast I couldn't make but for heads or tails of it all, but it went down so fast the world I thought I lived in went from earthly to some ethereal dreamscape, and just like that everything stopped.

It took me a spell to get my bearings but when I did, I was alone in this dark place...I felt around bumping into squishy things along the way, feeling this and that, finally a burst of light flashed on. I walked toward it, it was a bright white light...What the hell?

I looked behind me, everything was all dark and spooky. So I moved toward the light...It was warm, and comforting, and then I saw the sides of the world I was in. There was doctors and nurses. There was all this equipment like in a hopital...Howee! I was in a hospital, and I was in a body, and that body was hooked up to a bunch of tubes and machines, and then I heard someone say: "He's gone."

Someone else said: "Time of death..."

I didn't right get the time, but knew with every bit of my thinker brain that I was in the body of someone who'd died, and that someone wasn't goin' to hell, no, they done seen the bright white light that'd been illusive to me twice before. Hellsfire, I was ridin' a beam of light to the other place...What the hell?

I was transplanted for no rhyme or reason on a ship sailin' toward uncharted territory...Could all my good deeds spun around, did I take someone else's seat on trip to heaven? I had to jump out of the eyeball, and jumped hard up against it, but landed in a pool of pure luminescent energy, and rode the beam like a bronkin' buck toward wherever it was gonna take me...

And then everything went to a stop, and the world I saw through my seein' eyes went blurry, and there I was sittin' before some shape...It coulda been a person, but they was glowin' like a lighting bug in a jar. He was sittin' in a tuft of clouds like some judge was there, and was about to pass sentence. Then I heard a voice say this:

"Hello Mr. Seeney. I see you have managed to sneak into heaven. You had best make yourself comfortable there are a lot of questions that remain to be answered."

About then I knew everything I'd learned was about to slip into forgetfullness land, and I'd done made a wrong turn on the cosmic highway...Hellsfire, I was the wrong man in someone else's body, takin' the place of somebody that needed to be where I was.

That's when I jumped...

AFTERWORD
Trip Wiley

I got back to the office at the Soul Salvation Center, and Eustice had left me an envelope with a wax seal. There was a Post It note on it that said: Open up if I don't come back in a week, in Eustice's scrawl. It had been a week, and I'd been out on a bender. I broke the seal with a letter opener and slit the top open. A gush of air burst out, and something in the room changed, the barometric pressure shifted like right before a storm, my ears began to tingle, and my hand shook. A wind kicked up and the windows rattled. Something was up, something not of this world. I removed a letter from who knows where, but it appeared to have come from some offical place. I felt around inside and removed a letter. It was the oddest paper I have ever seen, and the ink could have been blood, or some facsimile, but I had no question of its origin. No. I've been through too much with Seeney and his afterlife connections. The writing on the document was in a font like I've never seen, and after staring at it for several moments the caligraphy raised from the page...really, the letters of the words floated above the page and hung in the space before my eyes. I looked down, and the paper, if that's what it was, had disappeared leaving a fine dust that was picked up by the breeze and taken to a place I may never may know.

The letters spelled out words, and the words were few, but their meaning was clear. Eustice Seeney was hereby eighty sixed by the croupier of Hades, and was welcome into the domain of Heaven. Then the letters, faded into oblivion. And that was all that remained.

So in the end, Eustice got himelf into heaven. What happened *after* that is a whole different story. Wherever he is, I have no doubt he's going to be in a real heapatrouble.

HEAPATROUBLE